Disney · PIXAR
TOY
STORY

# ADVENTURES

## VOLUME 1

Dark Horse Books

**DARK HORSE BOOKS**

**PRESIDENT AND PUBLISHER** Mike Richardson

**EDITORS** Shantel LaRocque and Freddye Miller

**ASSISTANT EDITORS** Brett Israel and Judy Khuu

**DESIGNER** Anita Magaña

**DIGITAL ART TECHNICIAN** Christianne Gillenardo-Goudreau



**Toy Story Adventures Volume 1**


Published by Dark Horse Books
A division of Dark Horse Comics LLC.
10956 SE Main Street
Milwaukie, OR 97222

DarkHorse.com
To find a comics shop in your area,
visit comicshoplocator.com

First edition: April 2019
ISBN 978-1-50671-266-6
Digital ISBN 978-1-50671-283-3
10 9 8 7 6 5 4 3 2 1
Printed in China

DISNEY · PIXAR
TOY STORY
MASTER WOODY
SCRIPT: TEA ORSI
PENCILS: TERESA QUEZADA-GEER
INKS: MICHELA FRARE
PAINT: PACO DESIATO
ANDY GOT A PUPPY FOR CHRISTMAS AND SINCE THEN THE TOYS CAN'T LIVE IN PEACE.
BUSTER KNOWS THEY'RE ALIVE, BUT HE STILL TREATS THEM AS TOYS. HE LOVES THROWING, CHEWING AND SHAKING THEM!
THAT'S WHY THEY'VE BEEN TRYING TO PROTECT THEMSELVES FROM HIS ROUGH-AND-TUMBLE PLAY...
GREAT! THE **BARRICADE** IS ALMOST DONE!
SPR
OING
TRRR
COME ON, **CLUMSYSAURUS!**
SWISSS
VRRR
UHM...THESE BISCUITS ARE DIFFERENT FROM THE ONES WE USED LAST TIME, BUZZ?
VRRR

YEAH! JUST PUT THEM NEAR THE DOOR, **SHERIFF!**
OOOHKAY!

AND... **HUH?!** WHERE ARE YOUR NOSES?
THEY'RE IN A DRAWER!

WHY?!
THESE NEW BISCUITS **STINK!** WE CAN'T SMELL THEM!

MMM! I WISH I COULD PUT AWAY MY NOSE TOO!
COME ON, COWBOY!

THERE'S NO TIME TO LOSE!
**SHOOTING PISTOLS!**

A BIT LATER...
WHOA! IT'S **FANTASTIC!**
UHM...

ARE YOU SURE YOUR PLAN'S GONNA WORK, BUZZ?
OF COURSE!

WHEN **BUSTER** COMES IN, HE'LL EAT THE BISCUITS, THEN HE'LL FEEL TOO HEAVY AND TIRED TO JUMP THE BARRICADE AND PLAY WITH US!

**TIRED?!** WE'D NEED A WAGON OF BISCUITS TO MAKE HIM TIRED!

CALM DOWN, BUDDY! WE ARE PERFECTLY SAF...

WOOF WOOF

WOOF
UH-OH! HE'S COMING!
WOOF
TAKE YOUR POSITIONS! BUSTER'S HERE! 
QUICK!
LET'S MOVE!
HEEEEEELP!

WOOF
WOOF
HERE HE IS AGAIN!
SAVE ME, MY SUPER SPUD!

BRR! HE' SO SCAR-R-RY!
TLING
TLING
TLING
COULD YOU PLEASE STOP QUIVERING?

DON'T WORRY! I'M HERE!

LET'S SEE WHAT THE REAL DOG DOES...

CANINE ALERT! MAN YOUR BATTLE STATIONS!

PERFECT! HE'S GONNA EAT THE BISCUITS RIGHT AWAY!
?!

MAYBE BUZZ IS RIGHT...
SNIFF
SNIFF

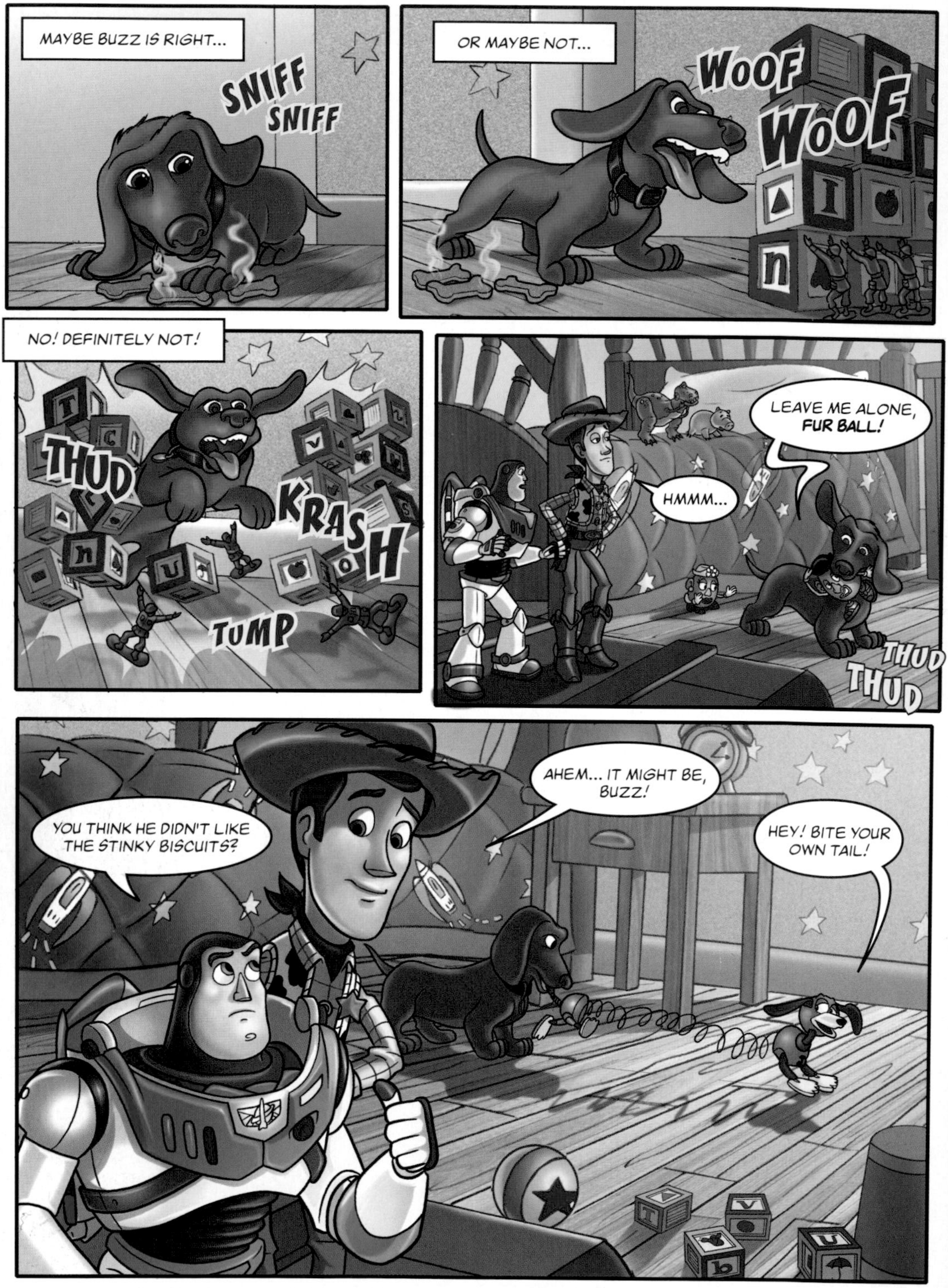

OR MAYBE NOT...
WOOF
WOOF

NO! DEFINITELY NOT!
THUD
KRASH
TUMP

LEAVE ME ALONE, **FUR BALL!**
HMMM...
THUD
THUD

YOU THINK HE DIDN'T LIKE THE STINKY BISCUITS?
AHEM... IT MIGHT BE, BUZZ!
HEY! BITE YOUR OWN TAIL!

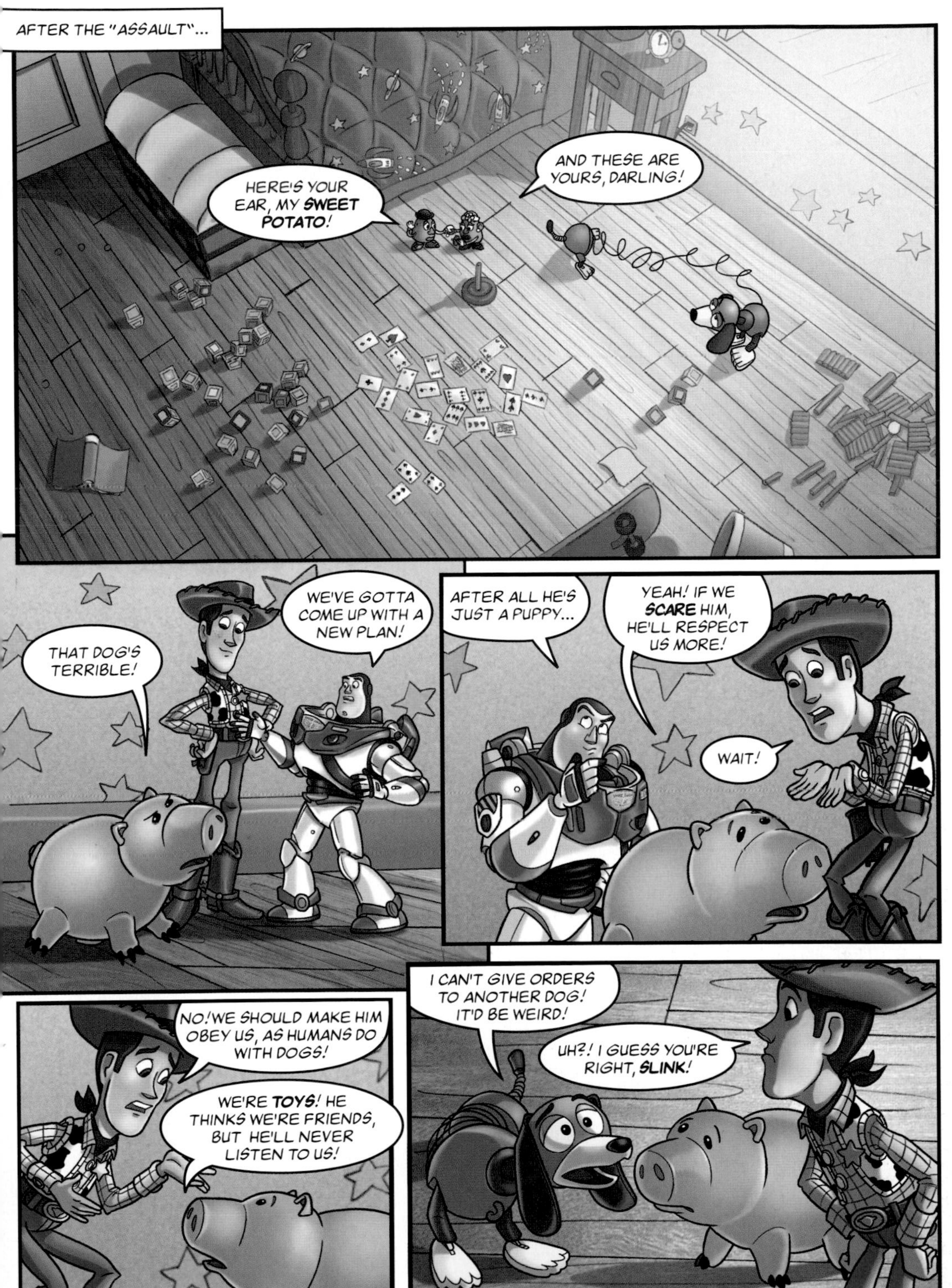
AFTER THE "ASSAULT"...
HERE'S YOUR EAR, MY **SWEET POTATO**!
AND THESE ARE YOURS, DARLING!
THAT DOG'S TERRIBLE!
WE'VE GOTTA COME UP WITH A NEW PLAN!
AFTER ALL HE'S JUST A PUPPY...
YEAH! IF WE **SCARE** HIM, HE'LL RESPECT US MORE!
WAIT!
NO! WE SHOULD MAKE HIM OBEY US, AS HUMANS DO WITH DOGS!
WE'RE **TOYS**! HE THINKS WE'RE FRIENDS, BUT HE'LL NEVER LISTEN TO US!
I CAN'T GIVE ORDERS TO ANOTHER DOG! IT'D BE WEIRD!
UH?! I GUESS YOU'RE RIGHT, **SLINK**!

DOGS ARE SCARED OF LOUD SOUNDS!

WE'LL MAKE A LOT OF NOISE AND HE'LL NEVER BOTHER US AGAIN!
I DON'T THINK IT'S THE RIGHT **SOLUTION**, HE...
**SHUT UP**, COWBOY! BUSTER WILL NEVER OBEY YOU!

LET'S FIND THE STUFF WE NEED!
WAIT! IT WON'T WORK!

WHY DON'T THEY LISTEN TO ME?! **SIGH**!
DON'T WORRY, WOODY!

WHEN BUSTER COMES BACK, THEY'LL FIND OUT YOU WERE RIGHT!
OH! THANK YOU, BO!

IN FACT, THE NEXT DAY...
DING
DONG BANG
?!
TRRR
TO INFINITY AND BEYOOOOND!
BONG
ARGH!

GRRRRH
DO YOU THINK HE'S SCARED?
AHEM...I DON'T THINK SO...

WOOOF
AAAH!
OH NO! BUZZ!!!
HIDE, FOLKS!

GASP!

OUCH!

SWISH
AAAH!

GRRRRRRRRRRH
NO, NO, NO!

PUT ME DOWN!
PLEEEEEEEEASE!
SWISH

WHOAAAA!

POOR WOODY!
BUSTER LIKES THIS NEW GAME!
WOOF

REACH FOR THE SKY!
TRRR

GASP! HE DID WHAT I SAID!
WHAT IS HE DOING?
MAYBE HE'S TIRED OF WALKING ON FIVE LEGS!

THAT'S HIS TAIL, BUZZ. DOGS HAVE FOUR LEGS!
REALLY?!
OH NO!

MY **HAT**!
WHAT SHALL WE DO?

STOP HIM!
COME ON, BUZZ, GO!
I CAN'T FACE HIM ALONE!

DON'T LOOK AT ME! I'M JUST A **TOY**!
YEAH, AND WE ARE **FURNITURE**!
**EXCUSE ME!**

COULD YOU PLEASE TAKE ME DOWN?
SURE, BUDDY!

MMM... IT'S STUCK!
**SIGH**! THAT'S JUST WHAT I NEEDED!

I'LL BE BACK WITH THE **BACKUP**!

**HERE** WE ARE!
WHAT...?!

REMEMBER! USE YOUR **POWER**!
OH...OKAY! I'LL BE STRONG AND BRAVE!

THWAK
ARGH!!

YAY! I DID IT!
COULDN'T YOU THINK ABOUT SOMETHING SOFTER?
COME ON! YOU'RE FREE, NOW!

WHAT WILL YOU DO ABOUT YOUR HAT, WOODY?
I'M GONNA FIND IT!
IT WON'T BE EASY, WOODY!
YEAH! I THINK BUSTER BURIED IT!
WHAT?!

HE'S IN THE YARD AND IS COVERED IN **MUD**!
YOU'LL NEVER KNOW WHERE YOUR HAT IS!

UNLESS I GET HIM TO OBEY ME ONCE AND FOR ALL!
C'MON, WOODY! WE TOLD YOU IT'S IMPOSSIBLE!
HE'LL SHAKE YOU AND CHEW YOU AS HE DID A MINUTE AGO!

BUSTER SEEMED TO LISTEN TO ME BEFORE...

HE STOOD UP WHEN I SAID: "REACH FOR THE SKY!"
UH?! THAT'S WHAT HE WAS DOING?!

I'LL GO AND FACE THAT PUP FOR OUR SAFETY...AND FOR MY HAT!
GOOD LUCK, MY HERO!

I'LL CALL YOU IF I NEED HELP!
OKAY, SHERIFF! GIVE HIM A LESSON!

IF HE LOSES, YOU'LL GIVE ME YOUR **CORK**!
AND IF HE WINS, I WANT YOUR **ANGRY EYES**!

THEN, IN THE YARD...

AHEM...EYES RIGHT, MAN! LET'S MOVE MOVE MOVE!
HE CALLED HIM MAN?!
RIDICULOUS!

SCRATCH
SCRATCH
UGH! I DIDN'T MEAN THAT!

TSK! DOGS ARE SO SILLY!
HEY, SHUT UP, PIGGY BANK!
BE STERNER, WOODY!

SIT DOWN! IT'S AN ORDER!
?!

WOOF
WOOF
PERFECT!

NO WAY! HE JUST WANTS TO **PLAY**...AS USUAL!
YOUR CORK IS MINE!
**GASP!**

HEY! WAIT A MINUTE!

**FIUUIT!**

**ARGH!** HE WANTS TO FIGHT HIM WITH THAT LITTLE TWIG!
**SSSH**, BUSTER'S LOOKING AT HIM!
**OUCH!**
BONK

FANCY PLAYING WITH ME, BOY?
ARF!

GO AND FETCH IT, DOGGY!
SWISSSS

YEAH! RUN! GOOD BOY!
WOOF
WOOF

WOW! THEY'RE PLAYING TOGETHER!
BAH! HE WON'T TAKE IT BACK TO HIM!
FETCH IT! I NEED MY CORK!

HEY! WELL DONE, DOGGY!

WHO'S A GOOD BOY? EH?! WHO'S A GOOD BOY?
PAT
PAT

TEE, HEE!
ARGH! HE WANTS TO EAT HIM!
SLAP
SLAP
NO! IT'S JUST DISGUSTING!

REACH FOR THE SKY!

GREAT JOB, BOY! EH, EH!
WOOF
SCRATCH
SCRATCH

HUH?! YOU WANNA PLAY AGAIN? OKAY!

AFTER MORE PLAYING AND MORE WATCHING...
OH DEAR! WHAT IS WOODY DOING NOW?
DUNNO! DO THESE EYES SUIT ME?
GRRR! I CAN'T EVEN LOOK ANGRY!

A FEW HOURS AGO, YOU BURIED MY HAT!
?!

PLEASE! CAN YOU DIG IT UP FOR ME?
?!

YOU DON'T UNDERSTAND ME, EH?

LET'S GO IN! I GUESS I NEED TO IMPROVE MY CANINE LANGUAGE!

BACK IN ANDY'S ROOM...
YOU WERE RIGHT, BUDDY!
YEAH! NOW WE'LL FEEL SAFER WHEN BUSTER COMES IN!
THANKS, GUYS!

I JUST WISH I MADE HIM GIVE ME BACK MY HAT!
WOO
WOOF
WOOF

WOOF
BUSTER?!
HE'S GOT YOUR HAT!

WOW! HE UNDERSTOOD WHAT I ASKED HIM, THEN!

GOOD DOGGIE!
WELL DONE, WOODY! YOU'VE FOUND YOUR HAT AND...YOU'RE A REAL MASTER NOW!

THE END

# HAMM'S WESTERN ADVENTURE

SO, YOU THINK YOUR PLAN WILL WORK?
SURE! IF ANDY SEES ME WEARING YOUR HAT, HE'LL SELECT ME AS YOUR COWBOY DEPUTY!

SHHH, HERE COMES ANDY NOW...

SOON...
IN THE DESERT, SHERIFF WOODY IS FIGHTING TO CAPTURE A NEW ENEMY...

HAMM... THE COW!
COW?!

MUCH LATER...
HEE, HEE... OKAY, I'LL UNTIE YOU, COW! ERR...I MEAN "COWBOY!"
HA. HA. VERY FUNNY!
HA HA HA HA!
THE END

SCRIPT: ALESSANDRO FERRARI; PENCILS & INKS: ETTORE GULA; PAINT: GIANLUCA BARONE.

# DINO-SCARE!

WOAH! THAT ROAR IS SOUNDING GREAT, REX!
GRRRAAAR!

THANKS, BUZZ! YOU'VE REALLY HELPED ME TO BE MORE FEARSOME!
WHAT ARE FRIENDS FOR? NOW, CROUCH IN LOW, SNARL YOUR TEETH, AND GRAB WITH THOSE PAWS...

YES! HERE, TAKE A LOOK...
GRRRAAAARRRR!

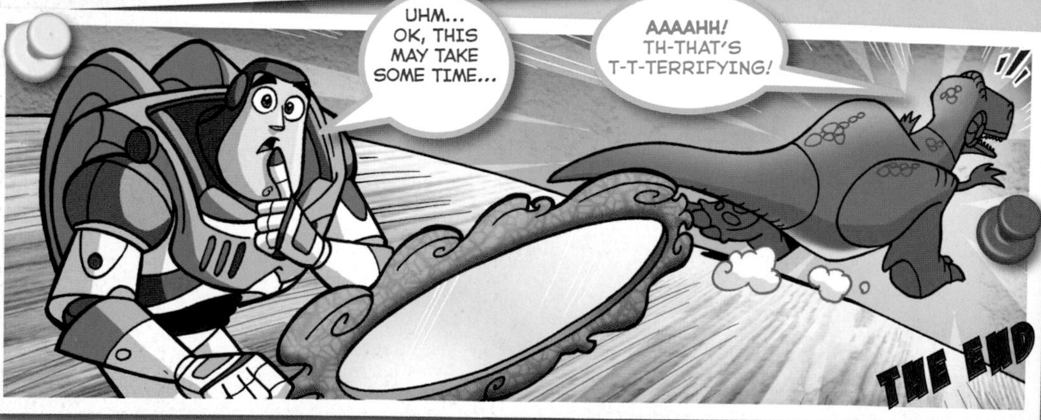

UHM... OK, THIS MAY TAKE SOME TIME...
AAAAHH! TH-THAT'S T-T-TERRIFYING!
THE END

SCRIPT: IAN RIMMER; PENCILS & INKS: ETTORE GULA; PAINT: GIANLUCA BARONE.

Disney · PIXAR
TOY STORY
A SCARY NIGHT
SCRIPT: TEA ORSI
PENCILS: AMY MEBBERSON, ANDREA GREPPI, AND VALENTINO FORLINI
INKS: FEDERICA SALFO
PAINT: PACO DESIATO
ANDY'S AWAY AT A SLEEPOVER AND...
WHAT A **BORING** EVENING!
WHAT COULD WE DO?
GO AND GET BORED ON ANOTHER **PLANET, SPACEHEAD**!
YEAH! WE CAN'T PLAY IF YOU KEEP COMPLAINING!
HOWDY! COME WITH ME, FOLKS!
WOODY!
WHAT'S UP, BUDDY?
OKAY! NO ONE WANTS US TO PLAY TONIGHT!
UMPF!

WHERE HAVE YOU BEEN, WOODY?
YOU'LL SEE SOON, BO!
AND SO...
WELCOME TO THE **TOY CAMP**!
IT'S A **CAMPFIRE**!
**WHOA!**
WELL DONE, SHERIFF!
YOU'VE GOTTA THANK THE **GLOW-BUGS** TOO!
OH! IT'S A PLEASURE!

AS EVERYONE SEEMED TO BE BORED, I THOUGHT WE'D HAVE A **CAMPOUT**!
OH! YOU'RE THE **BEST**, WOODY!
SMACK
C'MON! THIS IS CAMP, NOT A ROMANTIC DATE!
SHUT UP, YOU **GRUMPY SPUD**!
NO! THIS TIME THE POTATO'S RIGHT!
YEAH! LET'S DO SOMETHING PEOPLE USUALLY DO AT A **CAMPOUT**, LIKE...
LIKE...UH... LIKE...
HEY! **WHAT** DO PEOPLE USUALLY DO AT A CAMPOUT?
DON'T WORRY, BUZZ! I'M AN **EXPERT**!

WE COULD SING A SONG AROUND THE FIRE, FOR EXAMPLE!
YES, YES! LET'S SING A SONG!
THE BIG DINOSAUR RAN AWAAAAY...
ARGH!
GULP!
HE WAS LOOKING FOR A PLACE TO STAAAAY...
POP
HMM! SOMETIMES I WISH I WERE A POTATO HEAD TOO!
UM... REX! I THINK NO ONE FEELS LIKE SINGING TONIGHT!
?!
OR RATHER LIKE HEARING HIM SING!
HEY! WHY DON'T WE TELL SCARY STORIES?
NO WAY!

I BET NONE OF YOU CAN TELL A **TRULY** SCARY STORY!
?!

AND ANYWAY, **NO ONE** AND **NOTHING** COULD SCARE ME!
OH! MY **TOUGH** POTATO!
OOOHKAY, THEN!

IF WE DON'T TELL STORIES, YOU'LL HAVE TO LISTEN TO REX'S SONGS WITH YOUR EARS ON!
**GULP!**

OKAY! JUST TELL YOUR STORIES! I'LL HAVE A GOOD **LAUGH**!
YEAH!
I WANNA BE THE FIRST!

ONCE UPON A TIME, THERE WAS A **FEROCIOUS** DINOSAUR...

THIS IS GONNA BE GOOD! **TEE-HEE!**

"HIS TEETH WERE **HUGE** AND SHARP, AND..."

ROARRRRRRRR

"WITH HIS SHORT ARMS HE SCARED ALL THE OTHER... DINOSAURS!"

ROA... B-R-R-R!

B-R-R-R!
UM... WHAT'S WRONG, REX?

I CAN'T GO ON! I'M TOO SCARED!
!

C'MON! WHO'S GONNA TELL THE NEXT **JOKE**?
STOP BRAGGING, BUDDY!

MY STORY'S SO SCARY THAT IT'LL TURN YOU INTO A MASHED POTATO!

"MY COUSIN **SAUSAGE**..."
**SAUSAGE?**

YEAH! IT'S A VERY POPULAR NAME FOR PIGGY BANKS!
**OH?!** I SEE...

"ANYWAY... ONE DAY HE WAS MINDING HIS OWN BUSINESS WHEN SOMETHING TERRIBLE HAPPENED TO HIM!"

"HIS OWNER NEEDED SOME CASH TO BUY AN ICE CREAM CONE."

CRASH
"NO ONE TRIED TO GLUE HIS PIECES TOGETHER AGAIN."

SIGH! THIS IS SO SAD!
WHY DIDN'T THE GIRL SIMPLY OPEN HIS CORK?
WELL... I DON'T KNOW!

SORRY, HAMM! NO MASHED POTATOES FOR YOU TODAY!
OKAY! I'LL TELL YOU ANOTHER ONE!
GIVE IT UP, GUYS!
IT'S MY TURN NOW!

DID I EVER TELL YOU ABOUT MY MISSION ON **ALPHA BETAPHIN**?
YOU STUDIED THE **ALPHABET**?!

NO, REX! IT WAS EVEN MORE **DIFFICULT**!
OOOOOH!

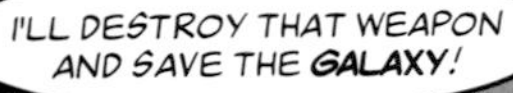
"THE STAR COMMAND HAD ORDERED ME TO GO TO **ALPHA BETAPHIN**, AN UNKNOWN PLANET WHERE THE EVIL EMPEROR ZURG HAD HIDDEN A TERRIBLE WEAPON!"
I'LL DESTROY THAT WEAPON AND SAVE THE **GALAXY**!

"AFTER A LONG, DANGEROUS FLIGHT, I REACHED THE PLANET..."
FSHHHH

OKAY! ZURG'S HIDEOUT SHOULD BE RIGHT THERE!
BIIP
BIIP

"AND FINALLY I FOUND ZURG'S BASE! IT WAS HUGE AND CREEPY!"

HERE IT IS!

YOUR STORY JUST MADE ME FEEL SLEEPY, BUZZ!
HUH?! IT'S JUST BECAUSE YOU'VE NEVER SAVED THE **UNIVERSE**!

YOU ONLY SAVED IT IN A VIDEO GAME, **SPACE GOOF**!
HEY! DON'T FORGET THE **TV SERIES**!
C'MON, FOLKS!

**ROCKY** WANTS TO TELL US HIS STORY!

AAAAH!
EEEEK!

YEAH! IT WAS GOOD, BUT CAMPFIRE STORIES ARE A BIT DIFFERENT!
C'MON THEN! WE HAVEN'T HEARD YOUR STORY YET!

OKAY! I WAS JUST ABOUT TO TELL IT TO YOU!

IT WAS A DARK AND GLOOMY NIGHT, AND I WAS AT COWBOY CAMP WITH ANDY ...

"HE WAS OUT FOR A BARBECUE AND I WAS ALONE IN THE CABIN...
RODEO

"BUT SUDDENLY A CREEPY NOISE SCARED ME... JUST A LITTLE BIT, OF COURSE!"
WHOOOOOOOOOOOOO
ARGH!
BONK

"MY HEAD SMARTED BUT I **WASN'T** SCARED..."
WHOOOOOOO
OUCH!

"SO I DECIDED TO HAVE A LOOK OUTSIDE..."
LET'S SEE WHO'S MAKING ALL THIS NOISE!
ANDY

MMM...IT'S TOO **DARK**! I CAN'T SEE ANYTHING!

WHOOOOOOO
!

WHOOOOOOOOOOOO
AAAAAAAAAAAH!
THUD

WELL DONE, COWBOY! I BET YOU GAVE THE **OWL** A GOOD LESSON!
UM...**NO**...

ACTUALLY, I JUST **FELL OFF** THE WINDOWSILL!
I'VE HAD ENOUGH OF YOUR **LAME** TALES!

HAVE YOU EVER HEARD OF THE **ONE-ARMED TOY KIDNAPPER**?
N-NO!
C'MON, REX! IT'S JUST A STORY!

YOU WON'T SAY THAT AFTER LISTENING TO IT, BO PEEP!
**OH!**

GET READY FOR SOMETHING **TRULY** SCARY!

"A FEW YEARS AGO SOME KID'S TOYS STARTED DISAPPEARING...

"SOMEONE TERRIBLE WAS TAKING THEM AWAY...

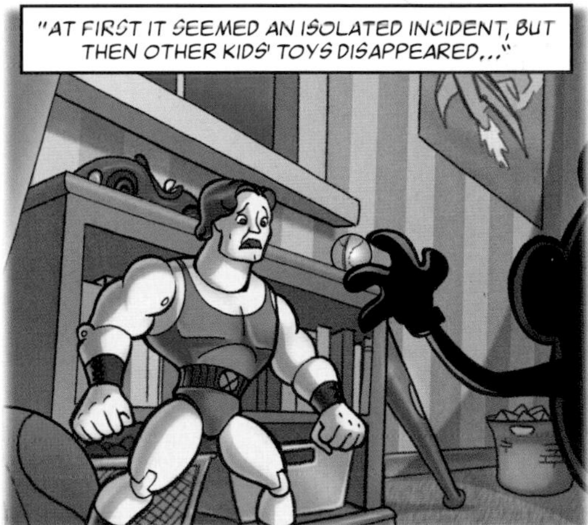
"AT FIRST IT SEEMED AN ISOLATED INCIDENT, BUT THEN OTHER KIDS' TOYS DISAPPEARED..."

THE KIDS THOUGHT THEY'D JUST LOST THEIR TOYS!

"BUT THE TOYS KNEW IT WAS SOMETHING WORSE AND WERE ON ALERT...

"ANYWAY, IT WASN'T ENOUGH!"
AAAH!
SNATCH

"RUMORS SPREAD IT WAS THE ONE-ARMED TOY KIDNAPPER.
"HIS OWNER HAD LOST ONE OF THE TOY'S ARMS, AND THE TOY WAS ANGRY THAT HE WASN'T BEING PLAYED WITH ANYMORE."

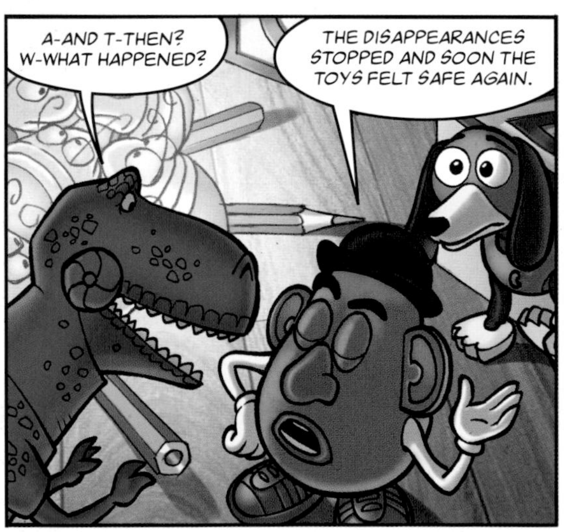
A-AND T-THEN? W-WHAT HAPPENED?
THE DISAPPEARANCES STOPPED AND SOON THE TOYS FELT SAFE AGAIN.

PHEW!
HOLD ON, SHERIFF! THE ONE-ARMED KIDNAPPER'S STILL OUT THERE!

I'M SURE ABOUT IT!
BECAUSE IT'S ME!
SHOOTING PISTOLS!
HEEEELP!
ARGH!
EEEEEEW!
POP
YA SEE?! THAT'S HOW IT'S DONE!
!
YEAH! I'VE GOT TO ADMIT THAT WAS GOOD!
BUT NOW IT'S TIME TO GO TO BED!

GOOD NIGHT, BO!
'NIGHT, WOODY!

YOU CAN TURN YOUR LIGHT OFF, THANK YOU!

BUT...
FRUSSSSSSSSSH

GULP! WHAT WAS THAT NOISE?
BLIP
REX, HAMM, IS IT YOU?

NO, WE'RE BOTH HERE!
P-PLEASE! DON'T LEAVE ME ALOOOONE!

URGH!
FRRRRRRRRUSH
HEY! IT'S COMING FROM UNDER THE BED!
YOU'RE RIGHT!

OKAY, THEN! LET'S GET TO THE BOTTOM OF THIS!

C-COME OUT, IF YOU DARE TO!
GRRRRRRRRRRH
GROWL

WHOAAA!
HOLD ON, SHERIFF!

SNAP

AAAAAHHH!
ANDY

WHATEVER'S UNDER THERE DOESN'T LIKE PENCILS!
ANDY

M-MAYBE IT'S B-BUSTER!
NO!
YEAH! THAT DOG IS A PEST!
ANDY

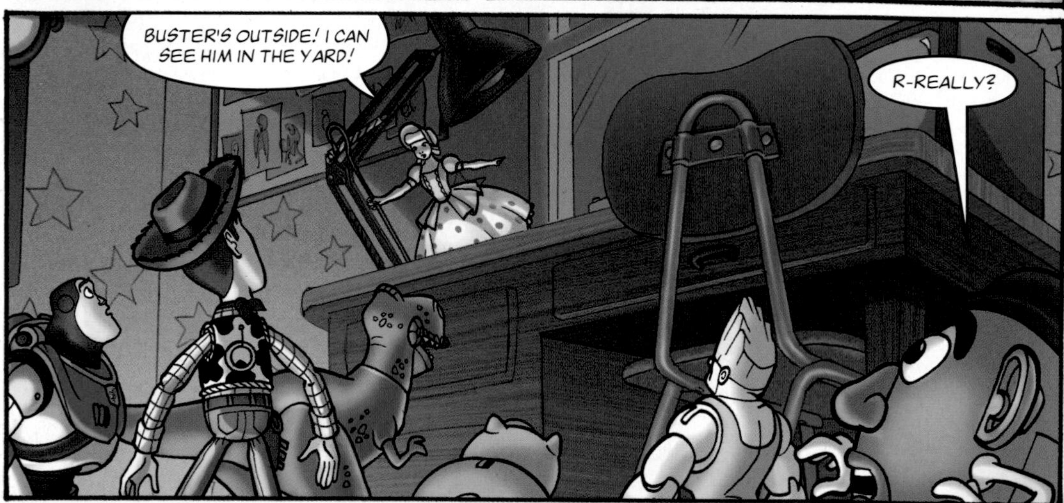
BUSTER'S OUTSIDE! I CAN SEE HIM IN THE YARD!
R-REALLY?

DON'T TELL ME YOU'RE SCARED!
NO WAY! I TOLD YOU THAT... UH... NOTHING SCARES ME!

HMM... WE NEED A PLAN!
I HAVE ONE...

LET'S RUN AWAY!
UMPF!

RC!
WELL DONE! THE FLASHLIGHT WILL HELP US SEE UNDER THE BED!
VRRR

YOU CAN GO WITH HIM, MR. POTATO!
W-WHY ME?

YOU SAID YOU'RE NOT AFRAID! DIDN'T YOU?!
GRRRRRRR
FINE...UM... NO PROBLEM! I'LL GO!

YOU'RE MY HERO!
C'MON! SHOW YOURSELF...UH... MONSTER!
WOOF WOOOF
SPROING
URGH!
SLINK?!
AAAAAAAAAAAHHHHH!
WELL...WAS IT SCARY ENOUGH FOR YOU?
NO...UM...I WASN'T SCARED AT ALL!
WHAT?! YOU ALMOST JUMPED OUT OF YOUR POTATO SKIN!
HUH?! GROAN! TOMORROW WE'LL JUST PLAY CARDS, OKAY?!
YEAH! I THINK IT'S ENOUGH SCARING FOR ONE NIGHT! HEE-HEE!
THE END

STORY CONCEPT: SERGIO BADINO; SCRIPT DEVELOPMENT: ALESSANDRO FERRARI; PENCILS & INK: ETTORE GULA; PAINT: GIANLUCA BARONE.

OH,NO! THIS THING IS BROKEN AGAIN...

!
THAT'S IT! TIME TO GET A NEW ONE!

EMERGENCY! SARGE'S BEEN SUCKED UP!
!?
WHAT? SARGE?

AND SO, AFTER THE NECESSARY EXPLANATIONS...
REX SAYS SARGE'S IN THE BELLY OF THAT TOYSUCKER...

...RESCUING HIM WON'T BE EASY!

KEEP COOL, BUZZ. ETCH-A-SKETCH AND I HAVE COME UP WITH THE PERFECT PLAN!
UMM... I THINK YOUR PLAN JUST GOT OUTDATED!
HUH?
IN TWO WORDS: GARBAGE TRUCK!
EMERGENCY PLAN C24, SOLDIERS! ON THE DOUBLE!
AT YOUR COMMAND, SHERIFF! MOVE OUT, MEN!
REX, HAMM, TAKE THIS! DON'T REWIND IT UNTIL WE'VE TIED IT TO THE VACUUM CLEANER!
WAIT FOR OUR SIGNAL, OK?

READY, PAL?
READY AS EVER! WE'RE SKYWARD BOUND...
VVRROOOMMM!
...AND BEYOND!
TARGET IDENTIFIED... LET'S MAKE IT A SOFT LANDING, SPACE RANGER!
WAAAA!
SOFT LANDINGS CAN BE PRETTY HARD!
SBAM!

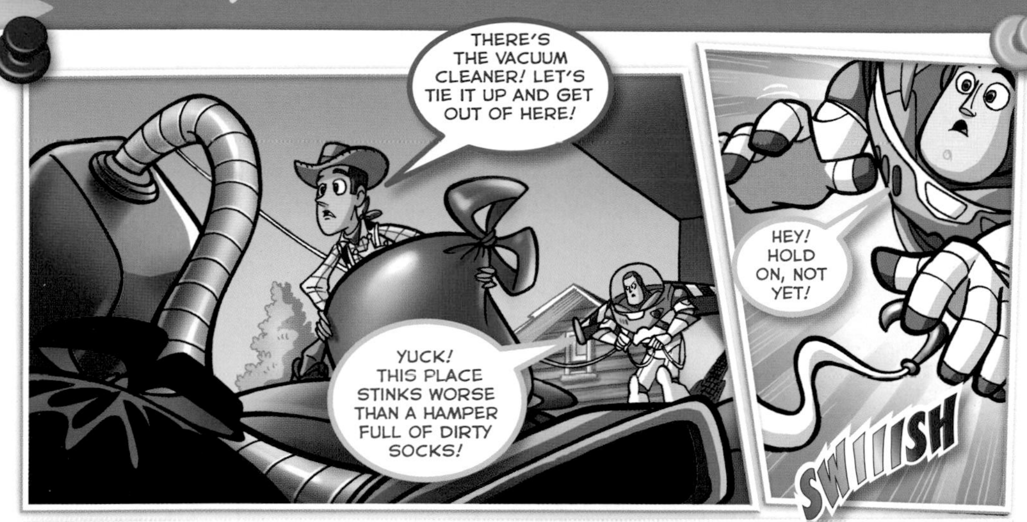
THERE'S THE VACUUM CLEANER! LET'S TIE IT UP AND GET OUT OF HERE!
YUCK! THIS PLACE STINKS WORSE THAN A HAMPER FULL OF DIRTY SOCKS!
HEY! HOLD ON, NOT YET!
SWIIIISH

HOW EXACTLY DID YOU INTERPRET THE WORDS, "WAIT FOR OUR SIGNAL?"
OOPS.
SWIIISH

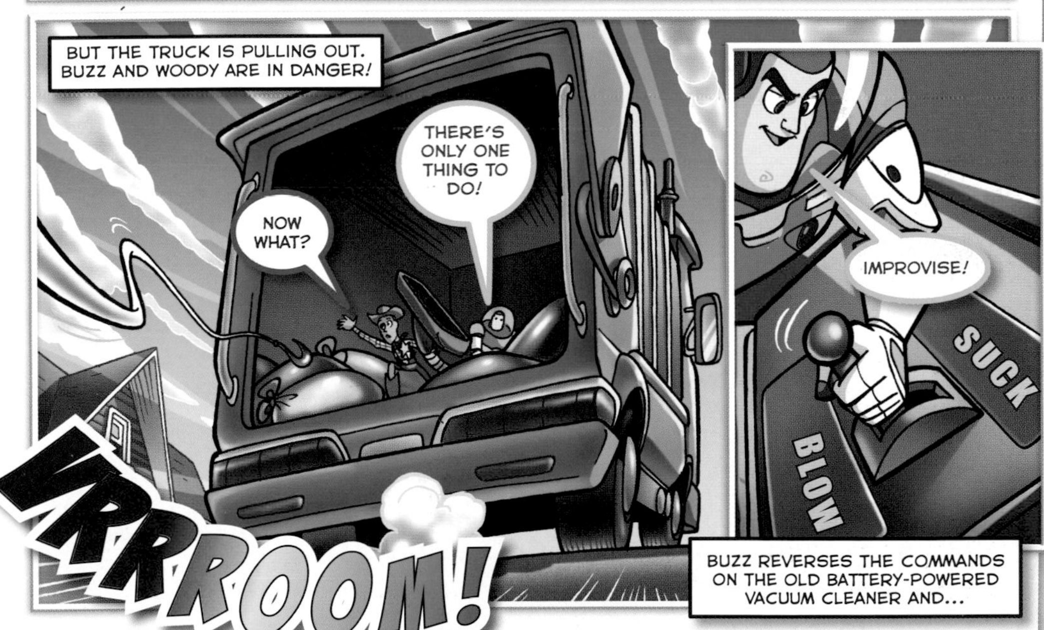
BUT THE TRUCK IS PULLING OUT. BUZZ AND WOODY ARE IN DANGER!
NOW WHAT?
THERE'S ONLY ONE THING TO DO!
VRRROOM!
IMPROVISE!
SUCK
BLOW
BUZZ REVERSES THE COMMANDS ON THE OLD BATTERY-POWERED VACUUM CLEANER AND...

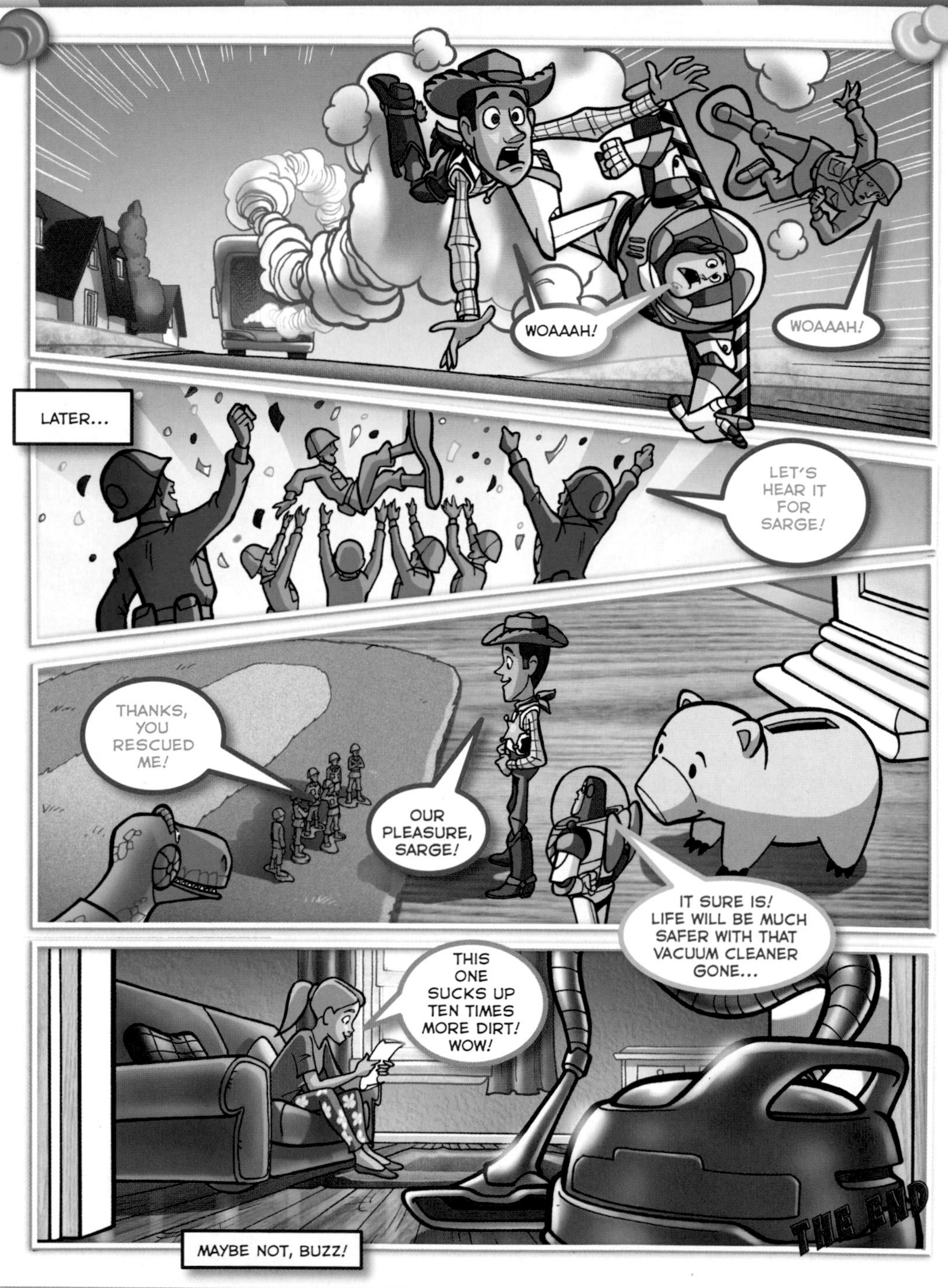
WOAAAH!
WOAAAH!
LATER...
LET'S HEAR IT FOR SARGE!
THANKS, YOU RESCUED ME!
OUR PLEASURE, SARGE!
IT SURE IS! LIFE WILL BE MUCH SAFER WITH THAT VACUUM CLEANER GONE...
THIS ONE SUCKS UP TEN TIMES MORE DIRT! WOW!
MAYBE NOT, BUZZ!
THE END

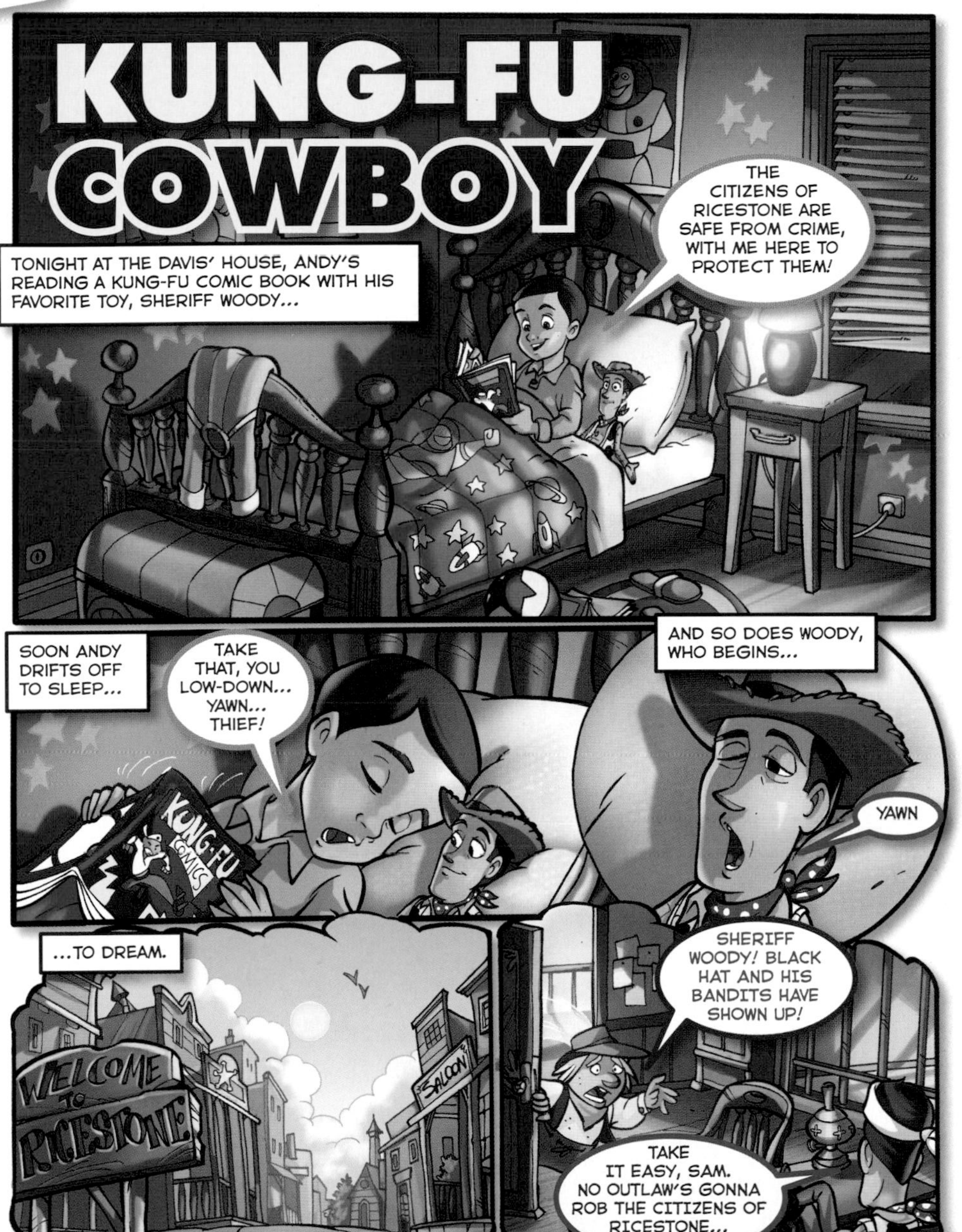


SCRIPT: ALESSANDRO FERRARI; PENCILS: LUCA USAI; INK: FEDERICA SALFO; PAINT: KAWAII CREATIVE STUDIO

...WITH ME HERE TO PROTECT THEM!
HAND OVER ALL THE MONEY IN TOWN, SHERIFF!
I'VE GOT BUT ONE THING TO SAY TO YOU, BLACK HAT...
...TAKE THAT! WAAAH!
POW
WHAM
WACK
THANKS, WOODY! YOU'RE OUR HERO!
JUST DOIN' MY JOB, FOLKS...

BUT THE NEXT MORNING, WHILE ANDY'S AT SCHOOL, WOODY'S WONDERFUL DREAM IS INTERRUPTED BY A REAL CALL FOR HELP!
EMERGENCY!
?!
RED MONKEYS ON THE LOOSE!!!
HELLLLLLP!
NO PROBLEM! THIS IS A JOB FOR THE KUNG-FU SHERIFF!
...OOOOH...
BOING
TONK
BAM!

WOODY! ARE YOU ALL RIGHT?
AW... I'M SO BAD AT FLYING KICKS!
WHAT ARE YOU TALKING ABOUT?
IF BANDITS COME, YOU WILL NEED A REAL KUNG-FU COWBOY, AND I'M NOT!
BUT YOU DON'T NEED FLYING KICKS TO BE A REAL GOOD COWBOY!
YOU THINK SO, BO?
SURE! THAT'S WHY YOU'RE OUR SHERIFF!
THE BEST ONE IN THE BUSINESS!
I'LL SAVE YOU, REX! WESTERN STYLE!
AAAAH!
THE END

DISNEY · PIXAR
TOY STORY 2

# CUDDLES, ANYONE?

BUSTER IS WOODY'S TRUSTY "STEED"... AND CRAVES LOVE AND AFFECTION...
GOOD BOY, GOOD BOY!
PAT PAT

BUT SOMEONE ELSE IS JEALOUS...
HEY! WHY THE LONG FACE, BULLSEYE?!

SCRATCH
YOU WANT SOME CUDDLES TOO, DON'T YOU?!

ARF! ARF!
SIGH! LOOKS LIKE I HAVE NO CHOICE.

SO TO KEEP THEM BOTH HAPPY...
THERE YOU GO, BOYS!
PAT
SCRATCH
THE END

SCRIPT: TEA ORSI; PENCILS: VALENTINO FORLINI; INK: MICHELA FRARE; COLOUR: KAWAII CREATIVE STUDIO

DISNEY PIXAR
TOY STORY 2

# WOODY'S STAR

SHERIFF

WHAT ARE YOU LOOKING FOR, WOODY?

I'VE LOST MY STAR DEPUTY BADGE!

A SHERIFF ALWAYS HAS TO HAVE HIS STAR!

SWIPS

YEEEOW!

UGH! NOW I SEE LOTS OF STARS!
HA! HA! HA!
THE END

SCRIPT: CARLO PANARO; PENCIL: VALENTINO FORLINI; INK: MICHELA FRARE; PAINT: KAWAII CREATIVE STUDIO

DISNEY · PIXAR TOY STORY 2

# SURPRISE RODEO

SCRIPT: SILVIA LOMBARDI; PENCILS & INK: ETTORE SULA; PAINT: KAWAII CREATIVE STUDIO

POP!
HELP!

HEY! WHAT ARE YOU DOING JUST STANDING THERE? HELP ME!
THERE'S ONLY ONE THING TO DO...

... PULL!
OOOH, **HEAVE!** OOOH, HO! OOOH...

OOF!
THE SITUATION IS MORE COMPLICATED THAN THE TOYS THOUGHT. WHAT THEY NEED IS A PLAN OF ATTACK!
WE SHOULD...
I THINK...
UGG!
WHAT IF...
HA! HA! HEE! HEE!
KEEP YOUR CHIN UP, COWGIRL! WE'LL SAVE YOU!
HEY! THANKS, PAL!
HEE! HEE!
HEY!!! THIS PLANT'S TICKLISH!
KEEP TICKLING WITH THAT TAIL, SLINKY. I HAVE A PLAN.

SLAP!
WELL, NOT EXACTLY WHAT I HAD IN MIND, BUT...
OOOOH!
...NOT BAD AFTER ALL! WHO WANTS THE NEXT RODEO RIDE?
NO, THANKS! I'M HAPPY JUST WATCHING!
M-MAYBE A LITTLE LATER, I'M BUSY NOW...
I'VE ALREADY HAD ENOUGH. HEE! HEE!
COUNT ME IN, COWBOY, THAT RIDE LOOKS **WILD!**
THE END

# WHERE ARE BUZZ AND JESSIE?

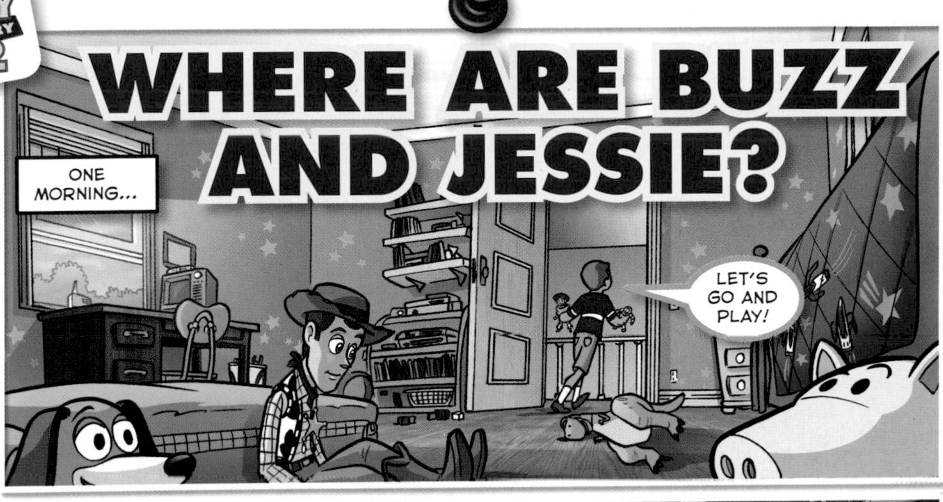

ONE MORNING...
LET'S GO AND PLAY!

TWO HOURS LATER, ANDY LEAVES WITH HIS MUM... BUT BUZZ AND JESSIE ARE NOWHERE IN SIGHT.
WHAT HAPPENED TO THOSE TWO?!

GENERAL MEETING!
BUZZ AND JESSIE HAVE DISAPPEARED!
SO HAS MY EAR!
SHH! THEY COULD BE IN TROUBLE!

LOOK EVERYWHERE AND KEEP ME INFORMED!
YES-SIR, SIR!

SCRIPT: TEA ORSI; PENCIL: VALENTINO FORLINI; INKS: MICHELA FRARE; PAINT: MARA DAMIANI

SARGE AND HIS SOLDIERS LEAD THE SEARCH...
EVERYBODY STAY TOGETHER!

WE'LL SEARCH EVERY CORNER OF THIS ROOM. YOU NEVER KNOW!

ONLY DIRTY SOCKS HERE!
YUCK!

ONLY COMIC BOOKS HERE...

SOMEONE ELSE IS A LITTLE LUCKIER...
MY MISSING EAR!

THEN SUDDENLY...
WE'VE FOUND 'EM!

WHERE ARE YOU?
IN FRONT OF THE BATHROOM DOOR! BRING A ROPE!

THE REST OF THE TOYS ARRIVE ON THE SCENE...
YEEE!
WHOA!
THEY'RE LOCKED INSIDE!
SOUNDS LIKE THEY'RE IN TROUBLE!

AAAH!
LET'S MOVE! A BUBBLE MONSTER'S EATING THEM ALIVE!

SWOOSH!

CLICK!

HEAVE!

INSIDE THE BATHROOM...
OOOH!
OOOH!
?!
WH-WHO'S GOING TO SAVE THEM?!

THE SHERIFF, OF COURSE!

!!!

BUZZ AND JESSIE ARE IN NO TROUBLE AT ALL! THANKS TO ANDY, THEY'VE LEARNED A NEW GAME...
SHALL WE CALL IN REINFORCEMENTS, SIR?
UMM... NO... UNLESS THEY'D LIKE TO TAKE A MOTORBOAT RIDE TOO!
HEY, WOODY!
THIS IS AWESOME!
THE END

Disney · PIXAR

TOY STORY

# WATER RESCUE

EVERY YEAR, ANDY GOES TO SUMMER CAMP...

I'M READY FOR THE **BLUEBERRY PICKING**!!

IT'LL BE FUN!

LET'S GO!

BUT THIS TIME HE BROUGHT HIS FRIENDS WITH HIM...
**UHM**...I THINK THEY'RE GONE!


SCRIPT: TEA ORSI, PENCILS: ANDREA GREPPI, INKS: MICHELA FRARE, PAINT: PACO DESIATO

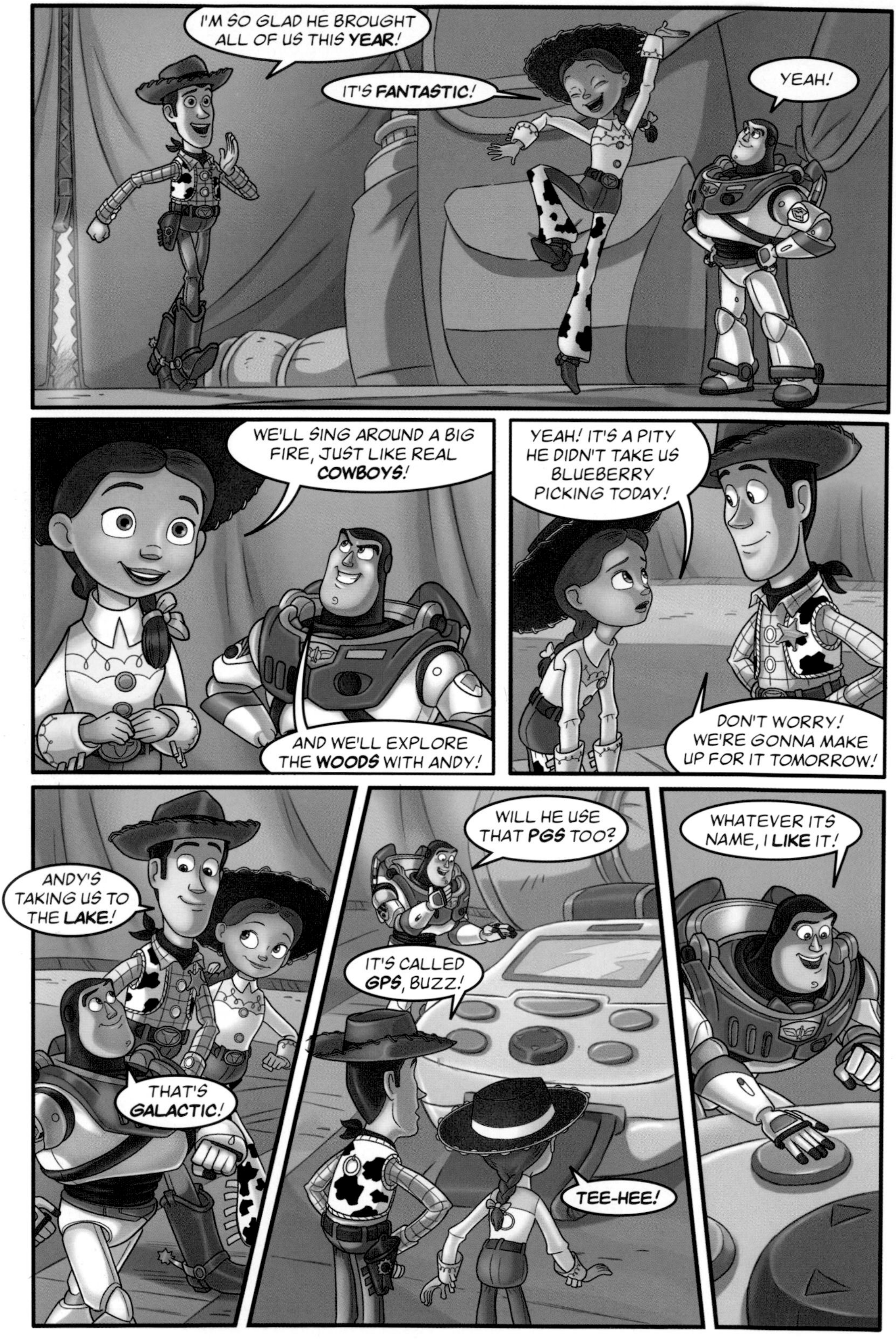

I'M SO GLAD HE BROUGHT ALL OF US THIS YEAR!
IT'S FANTASTIC!
YEAH!

WE'LL SING AROUND A BIG FIRE, JUST LIKE REAL COWBOYS!
AND WE'LL EXPLORE THE WOODS WITH ANDY!

YEAH! IT'S A PITY HE DIDN'T TAKE US BLUEBERRY PICKING TODAY!
DON'T WORRY! WE'RE GONNA MAKE UP FOR IT TOMORROW!

ANDY'S TAKING US TO THE LAKE!
THAT'S GALACTIC!
WILL HE USE THAT PGS TOO?
IT'S CALLED GPS, BUZZ!
TEE-HEE!
WHATEVER ITS NAME, I LIKE IT!

LET'S SEE HOW IT WORKS!
CLICK

CLICK
CLICK
CLICK

HEY! I THINK IT'S BROKEN!
NO! IT'S JUST **SWITCHED OFF**!
BUT IT DOESN'T WORK WELL INSIDE THE TENT!

IS THERE A BETTER WAY TO CHECK OUR DESTINATION, WOODY?
YEAH! WE COULD HAVE A LOOK AT ANDY'S **MAP**!

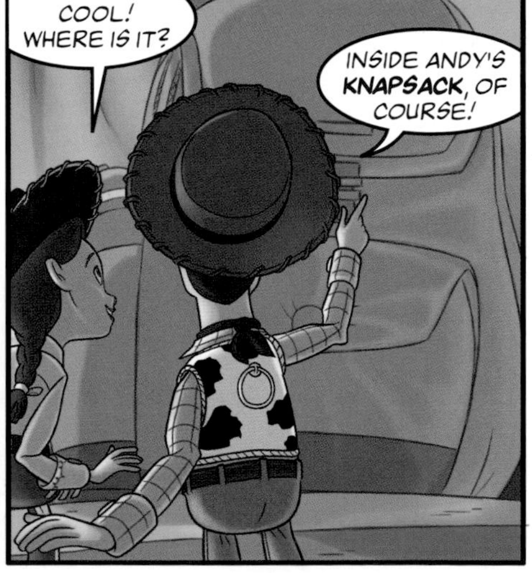
COOL! WHERE IS IT?
INSIDE ANDY'S **KNAPSACK**, OF COURSE!

WHOA! LET'S GET IT AND HAVE A LOOK!
SURE!
HOLD ON, FOLKS!

ANDY REALLY REALLY CARES ABOUT THAT MAP!
HE'LL BE VERY DISAPPOINTED IF IT GETS DAMAGED, SO...

YOU MUST PROMISE TO BE CAREFUL WITH IT!
!

THE MAP WILL BE SAFE WITH US, BUDDY!
I GIVE YOU MY COWGIRL WORD!

WELL... I GUESS I HAVE NO CHOICE!
HOORAY!
OKAY! LET'S GO!

GOOD! I'LL CLIMB THE KNAPSACK AND RETRIEVE THE MAP!
THAT SOUNDS LIKE A GOOD PLAN.

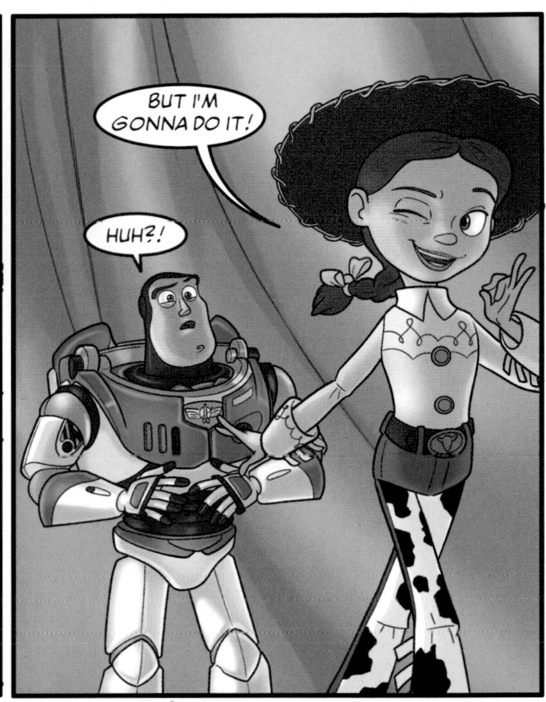
BUT I'M GONNA DO IT!
HUH?!

LET'S SEE...

HERE IT IS!

UGH...

OOOPS!
AHEM...JESS...
ARE YOU OKAY?

DON'T WORRY!
SWISS
?!

I'VE GOT THE **MAP**!
WELL DONE!
**WHOA!**

TAKE IT, GUYS!
WATCH OUT, BUZZ!

WE MUST HANDLE IT **CAR**-
**CAREFULLY**! I KNOW!

COME ON! I CAN'T WAIT TO SEE WHERE WE'RE GOING!
ME TOO!

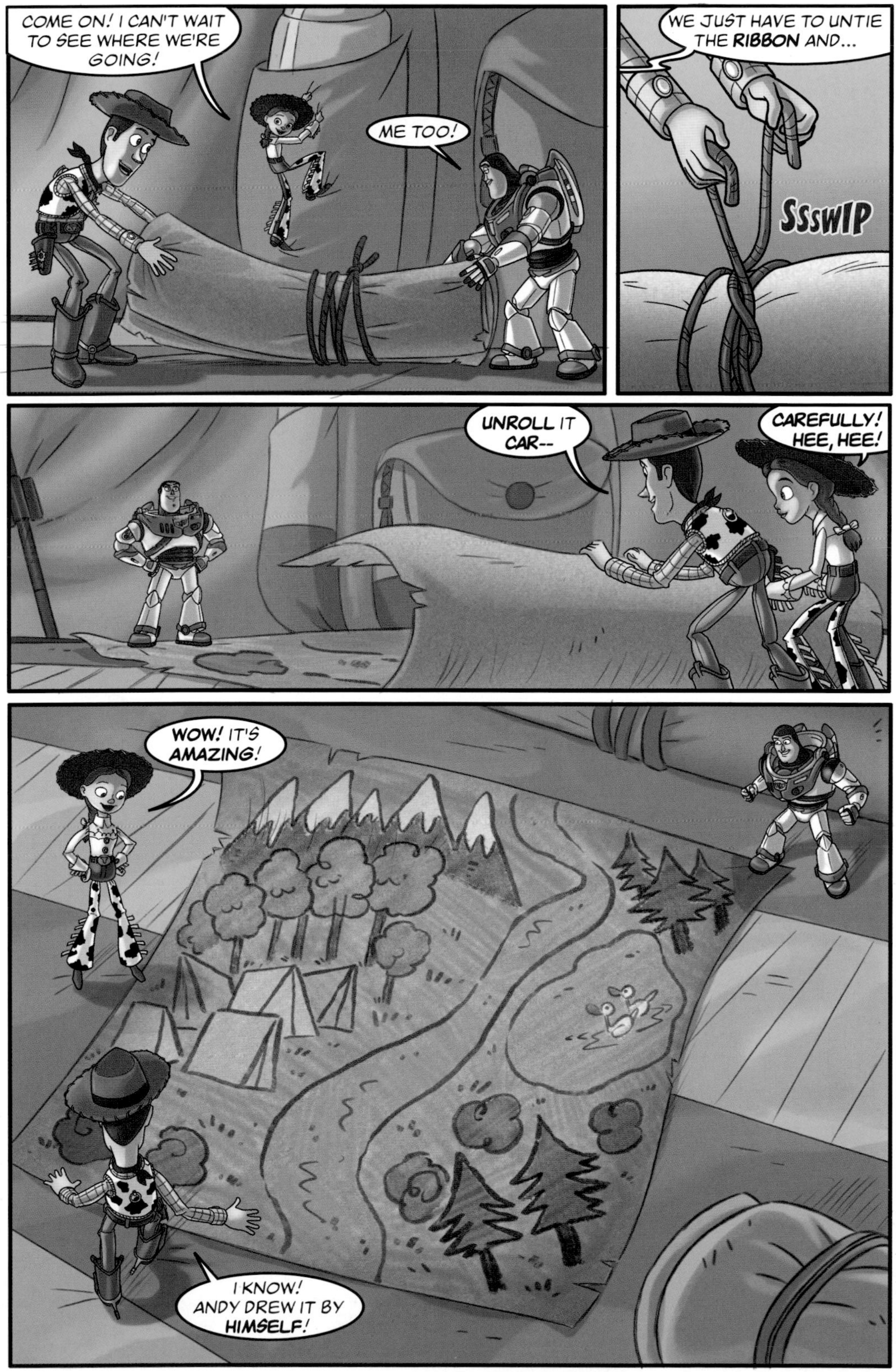

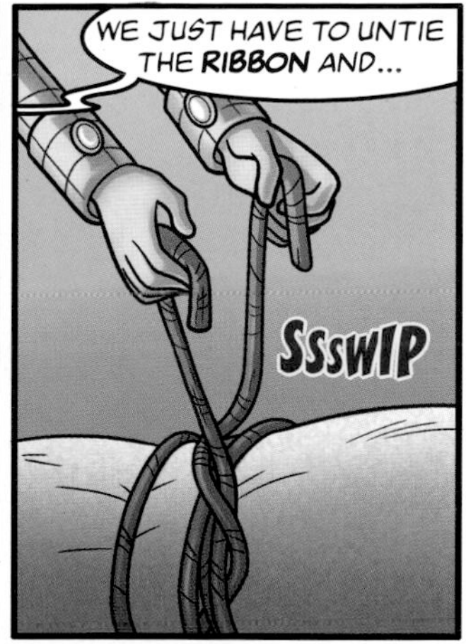
WE JUST HAVE TO UNTIE THE **RIBBON** AND...
SSSWIP

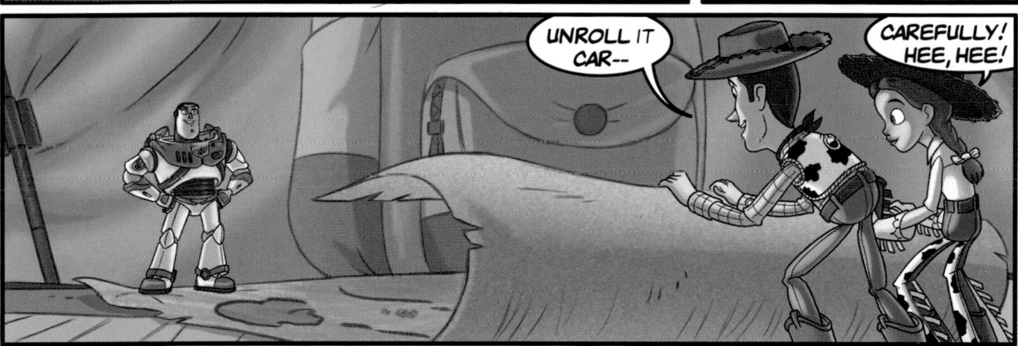
**UNROLL** IT **CAR--**
**CAREFULLY! HEE, HEE!**

**WOW!** IT'S **AMAZING!**
I KNOW! ANDY DREW IT BY **HIMSELF!**

AND HE CHOSE SUCH NICE COLORS!

THEY'RE SO BRIGHT, BUT IT'S TOO DARK IN HERE TO SEE THEM!
MAYBE WE CAN LIGHT UP THIS PLACE A BIT!

NO! I WON'T GO BACK INTO THE KNAPSACK TO GET THE LAMP!
NO WORRIES, JESS!

WE JUST NEED TO OPEN THE TENT'S DOOR!
HUH?!

ARE YOU SURE IT'S A GOOD IDEA?
C'MON! NO ONE WILL SEE US!

I'M READY!
WOODY! HELP ME, PLEASE!
UHM... OOOHKAY!

ANDY
BUT JUST FOR NOW WE NEED TO SEE THE COLORS!

PERFECT!
TUCK

LET'S SEE THESE COLORS NOW!
BE CAREFUL! YOU MIGHT RUIN IT!
FRRRR

RELAX, SHERIFF! YOUR MAP IS PERFECTLY SA-

ARGH!!
UH!
AAAHFE!
WOoooOOoSH

OH NO!
ANDY'S MAP IS FLYING AWAY!

SWIP
SWIP

I KNEW IT! WE SHOULDN'T HAVE TAKEN IT!
COME ON, WOODY! IT'S NOT OUR FAULT!
WE HAVE BEEN CAREFUL!

WELL... MAYBE NOT SO CAREFUL!

ANYWAY! THIS COULD'VE BEEN WORSE!
YEAH! THE MAP HASN'T FALLEN IN THE WATER AND IS NOT FAR FROM HERE!

HEY! MAYBE WE CAN RETRIEVE IT!
YEAH!
WE'LL SAVE THAT MAP!
CLAP

WE JUST NEED A SUPER-PLAN!

WHAT IF I LAUNCH MYSELF FROM THE TOP OF THE TENT?!
?!

"I'LL FLY ACROSS THE CANAL, AND...
ZZZZOT

"I'LL RETRIEVE ANDY'S MAP!"
MISSION COMPLETED!

GOOD PLAN, BUT...HOW WILL YOU GET BACK TO THIS SIDE?
UHM...I'VE GOT TO THINK ABOUT IT...

MAYBE YOU CAN SWIM!
NO WAY! THE MAP WILL GET WET!

UH! YOU'RE RIGHT!
SIGH! THERE MUST BE A WAY TO GET THERE...

HEY! I MIGHT HAVE FOUND IT!

WE CAN USE THAT BOARD TO SAIL ACROSS THE CANAL!
WOW! THAT'S EXCITING!
YEAH! I'VE NEVER BEEN ON A RAFT!

C'MON, THEN! WE'VE GOTTA GET MOVIN'!
YES! WE'RE A GREAT CREW!!

DON'T TELL HIM, BUT I'M THE CAPTAIN!
I HAD NO DOUBTS! TEE-HEE!
LIGHTYEAR

SO...
CARRY ON! WE ARE NEARLY THERE!
GOSH! IT'S HEAVY!

LET'S PUSH IT IN THE WATER!
SPLOSH

GET ABOARD, MY SAILORS!
I'VE GOT AN OAR!
GREAT! THAT'S JUST WHAT WE NEEDED!
SWISS

PLITSCH

RAISE ANCHOR! WE'RE READY TO **SAIL OFF**!
YAY!

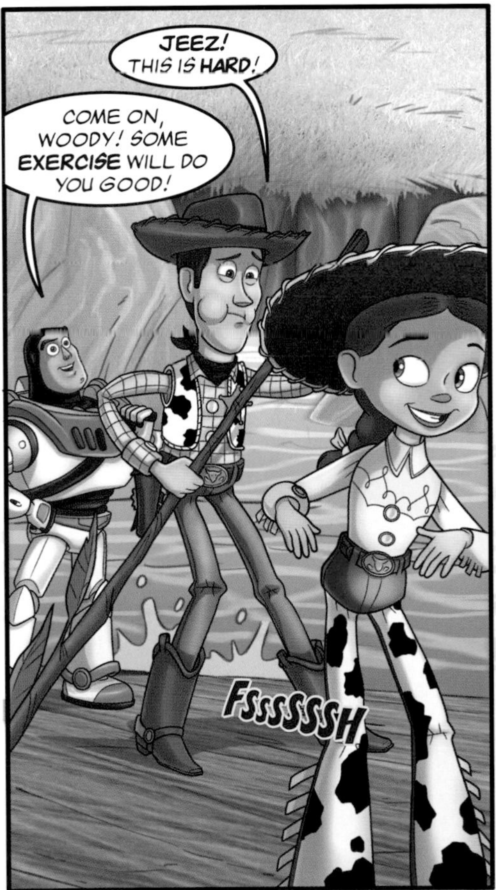
**JEEZ!** THIS IS **HARD**!
COME ON, WOODY! SOME **EXERCISE** WILL DO YOU GOOD!
FSSSSSSH

YEAH! AND IT'LL DO **YOU** EVEN MORE GOOD WHEN YOU ROW BACK!
AHEM... **SURE**!

**AH**! IT'S SO **LOVELY** TO BE SAILING ON THE WATER!
YEAH! HOPEFULLY WE'LL REACH THE MAP!

WHAT A GREAT IDEA, WOODY!
GULP!
SPAT

AAAAAAH!
THUD

TEE, HEE!
THIS IS NOT FUNNY! I COULD'VE FALLEN IN THE WATER!

I'M SORRY! I PROMISE I'LL KEEP QUIET!
DON'T WORRY, JESS! WE HAVE ANOTHER PROBLEM NOW...

HAVE YOU EVER BEEN CHASED BY A FISH?!
URGH!

YOU THINK HE WANTS TO EAT US?
WE JUST TASTE LIKE PLASTIC AND STUFFING, **MR. FISH**!
I D-DON'T KNOW!

I DON'T THINK HE CAN UNDERSTAND US, JESSIE!
BUT MAYBE WE SCARED HIM!

HE'S SWIMMING AWAY!
SPLASH
WOW! I THOUGHT WE WERE **FISH FOOD** FOR SURE!

AND WE'VE ALMOST REACHED THE OTHER SIDE!

TO INFINITY AND BEYOOOND!
PHEW! ALMOST THERE, WOODY!
PLITSH
PLOTSH

TUCK

NOW... HOW WILL WE GET THE MAP?!
GOOD QUESTION! THIS SIDE IS SO STEEP!

RELAX! BUZZ LIGHTYEAR CAN SOLVE ANY PROBLEM!

UGH! THESE ROCKS ARE SUPER-SLIPPERY! I CAN'T MAKE IT!
EVERY PROBLEM BUT THIS!

IF ONLY SLINK WERE HERE! HE COULD GET IT IN A JIFFY!
UHM...MAYBE I'M NOT AS STRETCHY AS HIM, BUT...

I CAN TRY TO DO SOMETHING!

ONCE THE PLAN'S BEEN EXPLAINED...
ARE YOU READY, WOODY?
YEP! HOLD MY RING TIGHTLY!
SAVE THAT MAP, SHERIFF!

TRRR

I'M ALMOST THERE!
GO, BUDDY, GO!
TRRRRR

I'LL GET IT!

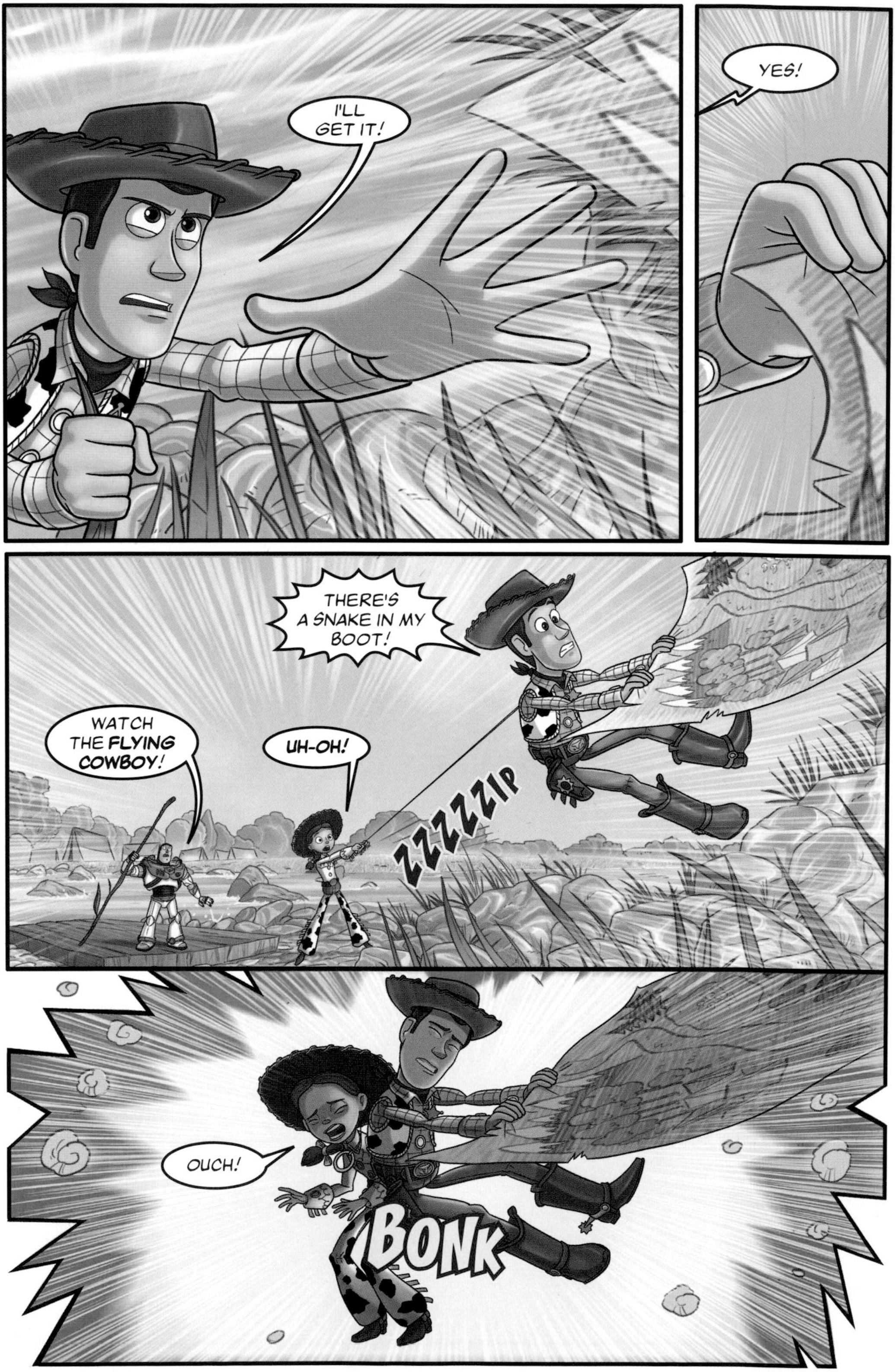

YES!

THERE'S A SNAKE IN MY BOOT!
WATCH THE **FLYING COWBOY**!
UH-OH!
ZZZZZZIP
OUCH!
BONK

WHOA! THAT WAS A GALACTIC COLLISION!

BUT ANDY'S MAP'S SAFE!
I'M SO HAPPY!!

TIME TO SAIL BACK, MY CREW!
STAK

LET'S GO, GO, GO! YIPPEE!
BE CAREFUL! THE MAP COULD GET WET!

RELAX, BUDDY! THE MAP'S SAFE NOW!
AHEM... I HOPE THIS TIME IT'S TRUE!
LIGHTYEAR

AND FINALLY...
PHEW! NOW IT IS REALLY SAFE!
I TOLD YA! HEE, HEE!
QUICK! ANDY'S COMING!

HI GUYS! I HAD A GREAT TIME!

TOMORROW I'LL PUT YOU IN MY KNAPSACK AND IT'LL BE EVEN MORE FUN!
ARE YOU READY FOR A NEW ADVENTURE, SHERIFF?!
SURE!

INSIDE ANDY'S KNAPSACK, WE'RE GONNA BE SAFE AND SOUND TOO!
WINK

THE END

# FRONT YARD ADVENTURE

SCRIPT: CARLO PANARO; PENCILS: LUCA USAI; INK: MICHELA FRARE; PAINT: MARA DAMIANI

I LIKE THAT PLACE... OOPS!
BUZZ!
BUMP
EVERYTHING OKAY, BUDDY?
NO PROBLEM, WOODY! I'M MADE OF TOUGH PLASTIC!
I'VE GOT TO GET BACK UP...
HISSSS!
AAAH!
BUZZ IS IN TROUBLE!

I'VE GOT TO HELP HIM!
WATCH OUT, WOODY!

HE WON'T BUDGE--I'M TRAPPED!

HIDE IN HERE, PAL!

HE DIDN'T SPOT US!

THE COAST IS CLEAR!
HISSSS!
AAAH!

THERE'S NO WAY OUT...

MY P-POOR FRIENDS...

GASP!

?!
THUMP!

AAAHHH!!!

YOU SAVED US, REX!
I WAS P-PRETTY SCARED...

BUT THE LIZARD WAS MORE SCARED THAN YOU!
REALLY?!
HA! HA!

THE END

DISNEY · PIXAR TOY STORY 2

# A THORNY RESCUE

REX LOVES ANDY'S NEW VIDEO GAME: SPACE HEROES...

GO, BUDDY! HIT THAT ALIEN!

NO! I'M TRYING TO AVOID HIM!

-LAST LEVEL
-JUMP
-STRIKE
-PUNCH

SEE? IT'S WRITTEN HERE!

WOW! ANDY'S TRICKS FOR FINISHING THE GAME!

SUDDENLY A GUST OF WIND BLOWS THROUGH THE WINDOW...

!

WATCH OUT, REX!

OH, NO!

-PUNCH

ALARM! ANDY'S NOTES HAVE BLOWN AWAY!

WELL, SHOOT MY PISTOLS!

ARGH!

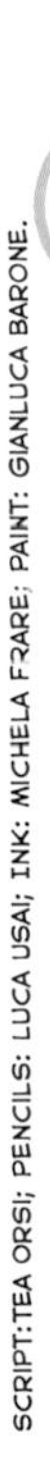

THEY'VE LANDED IN THE NEIGHBORS' FRONT YARD!
MAIL
-LAST LEVEL
-JUMP
-STRIKE
-PUNCH
GETTING 'EM BACK WILL BE CHILD'S PLAY!
UH-OH! THE MAILMAN MAY GET THERE FIRST!
-PUNCH
HE'S PUTTING THE NOTES IN THEIR MAIL-BOX!
-PUNCH
OH, NO! NOW WHAT?!
TAKE IT EASY! WE'LL GO GET 'EM!

ALL THAT'S NEEDED IS TRANSPORTATION...
PARPPP!

GOOD THING THERE'S BUSTER!
YEE-HA!
AAAH! COULDN'T WE CLIMB DOWN THE DRAINPIPE?!

UP WE GO!
UMM... GOT A PLAN B?

THESE THORNS MIGHT TEAR MY SPACE SUIT!
I DIDN'T COUNT ON THIS!

LUCKILY, WOODY'S A FAST THINKER!
?
UP ON YOUR HIND LEGS, BUSTER!

HOP UP ON MY SHOULDERS!
YES! AN INTERGALACTIC PYRAMID!
SO...
ALMOST THERE!
UGH! YOU WEIGH MORE THAN HAMM WITH A FULL BELLY!
-LAST LEVEL
-JUMP
-STRIKE
-PUNCH
THORNY RESCUE ACCOMPLISHED!
A LITTLE WHILE LATER...
GOOD JOB, GUYS!
HEE, HEE! THERE'S NOT A MISSION OUT THERE THAT BUZZ AND WOODY CAN'T TACKLE!
OKAY, BUT I'D SAY THAT'S ENOUGH RISK-TAKING FOR A WHILE!
-LAST LEVEL
THE END

# ETCH'S PRACTICAL JOKE

THANKS, ETCH!
?

HEY! CAN YOU DRAW ME TOO?

AHH!

HEY, THAT'S NOT ME!

HUH?! VERY FUNNY, ETCH!

THE END

SCRIPT: TEA ORSI; PENCILS: LUCA USAI; INK: MICHELA FRARE; COLOUR: KAWAII CREATIVE STUDIO

Disney · PIXAR TOY STORY 2

# THE COAST IS CLEAR

HOW'S THE SITUATION DOWN BELOW, SARGE?

NOBODY'S HOME! THE COAST IS CLEAR!

HEAR THAT? LET'S PROCEED WITH OPERATION S! S AS IN...

...S-S-S-SLIPPERY S-S-S-SLIDE!
HA! HA! AWESOME!
WHOOOOSH!

THE END

SCRIPT: CARLO PANARO; PENCILS: VALENTINO FORLINI; INK: MICHELA FRARE; COLOUR: MARA DAMIANI

Disney · PIXAR TOY STORY 2

# It's Party Time!

SCRIPT: TEA ORSI; PENCILS: LUCA USAI; INK: MICHELA FRARE; PAINT: KAWAII CREATIVE STUDIO

LATER ON, IN THE KITCHEN...
WELL? IS THIS GOING TO BE DIFFICULT?
DIFFICULT BUT VERY IMPORTANT!
WE NEED TO BRING BACK THE ALIEN GREEN STRAWS!
!!!
BUT WHY... ALIEN GREEN?
WE'RE MAKING OUTER SPACE DECORATIONS FOR OUR PARTY!
BUSTE
I NEED YOUR HELP! YOU'RE THE... BEST!
WELL... IF YOU PUT IT THAT WAY...
COMPLIMENTS WILL GET YOU EVERYWHERE! TEE, HEE!
GET MOVIN', BUZZ!

LET'S GET THOSE STRAWS!
I'M HERE, SUPER SHERIFF!
AND...
SWSSH!
TO INFINITY AND BEYOND!
WATCH OUT!
SPLASH!
NICE LANDING!
IT COULD HAVE BEEN WORSE! YUCK!
LATER...
WE'RE BACK, FOLKS!
PANT!

WELCOME TO OUR **WILD WEST** PARTY, SHERIFF WOODY!
YEE-HAA!
saloon
S
A
L
O
HEY! THIS IS BETTER THAN AN **OUTER SPACE** PARTY!
??!

THANKS, FRIENDS! THIS IS **GREAT!**
IT WAS TOUGH TO PULL OFF THIS SURPRISE, BUT WE DID IT!

BUT WHAT WILL I DO WITH THESE STRAWS?
I'VE GOT AN IDEA...

THIS **INTERGALACTIC** COWBOY BELT IS AWESOME!
A LITTLE TOUCH OF **OUTER SPACE** WORKS EVERY TIME! HA, HA!

THE END

# THE MYSTERIOUS TREASURE

SCRIPT: TEA ORSI; PENCILS: VALENTINO FORLINI; INK: MICHELA FRARE; COLOUR: KAWAII CREATIVE STUDIO

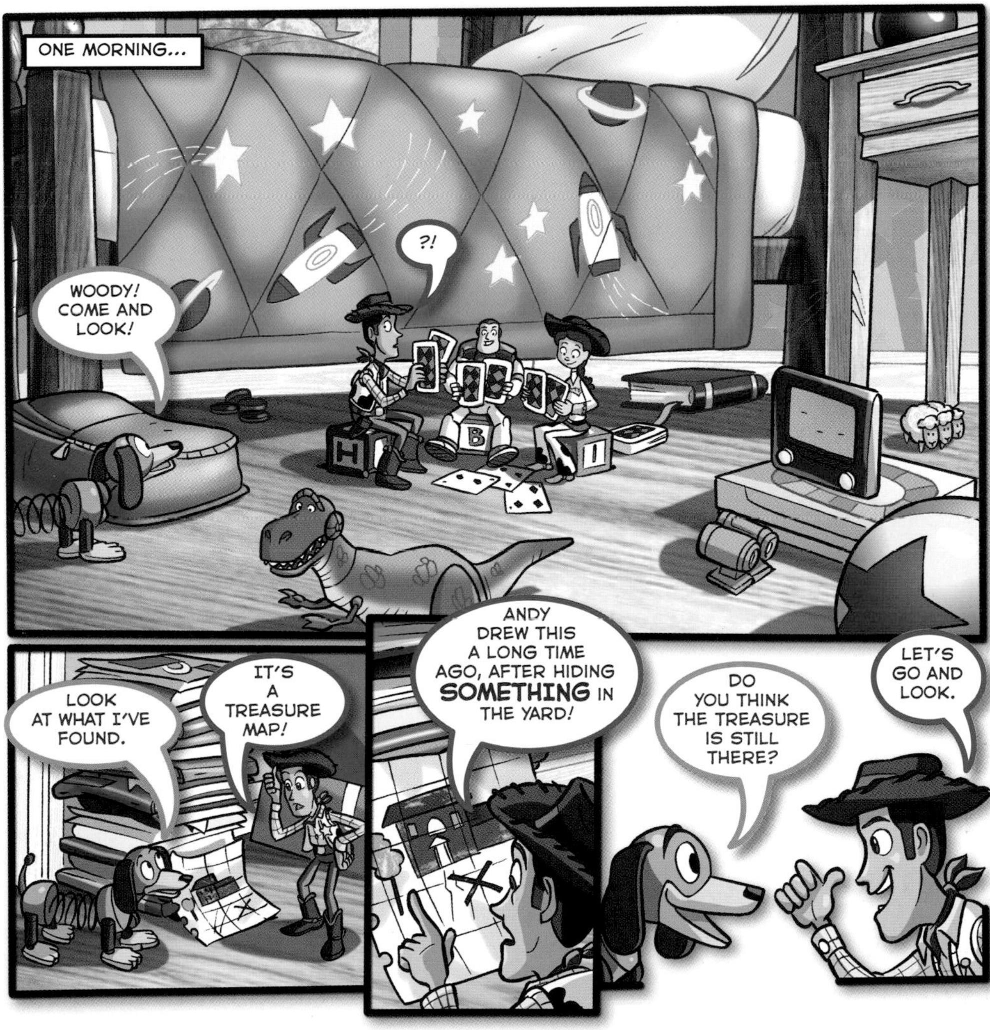

SO...
WHO WANTS TO HELP ME FIND THE TREASURE?
ME!
BUT I WANT TO GO.
LET ME GO. PLEEEEEEASE!
UM...
ER... OK THEN.
AND...
GOOD LUCK!
THANKS!
BUT SOON ENOUGH...
IT WON'T BE TRICKY TO FIND THIS TREASURE.
UM... I'M NOT SO SURE.
?
B-BEHIND YOU!
HISSSSS!

HISSSSS!
HELP!
OH, NO! WHAT CAN WE DO?
DON'T WORRY. I'VE GOT A PLAN.
OH DEAR.

AND WHAT A PLAN...
LOUDER, SLINKY!
GRRR, GRRR! WOOF, WOOF!
MEOOOW!

IT MUST BE UNDER HERE!

YEE-HA! THERE IT IS!
WOW!
CANDY

CLICK!
CANDY

HUH! WHAT'S THIS?
WE'LL SOON FIND OUT.

OH! IT'S BEAUTIFUL!
NOW THAT'S REAL TREASURE.
ANDY
WOODY

THE END

DISNEY • PIXAR

TOY STORY

# TO THE ATTIC!

ANOTHER ADVENTUROUS AFTERNOON IN ANDY'S ROOM...

YOU WON'T HAVE US, **CAPTAIN MASHED POTATO**!

WE'LL TAKE SHELTER IN THIS SECRET **BASE**!

WAIT! WE'RE COMING TOO!
TICK
TICK
TICK

**PHEW**! WE'RE SAFE NOW!
TUCK

SCRIPT: TEA ORSI, PENCILS: ANDREA ROSSETTO, INKS: FEDERICA SALFO, PAINT: PACO DESIATO

COME ON, SOLDIERS! WE'RE GONNA TAKE THAT BASE!

LET'S GO!
RIIIIING

ANDY! JIM AND HIS DAD ARE HERE!
COOL! I'M COMING!

THE FINAL BATTLE IS POSTPONED TO MONDAY, FOLKS!

I'M GONNA SPEND THE WEEKEND AT JIM'S COUNTRY HOUSE!
TOC

SEE YA LATER!

I THINK HE'S GONE!
OOOHKAY! LET'S GET OUT OF HERE!

TICK TICK TICK
WAIT! SOMEONE'S COMING!

UH! I ALMOST FORGOT ABOUT THE OLD MAGAZINES!

LET'S TAKE THEM UPSTAIRS!
FLIP

UGH! THEY'RE HEAVY!

SHRIEK
SHRIEK

THUD
?!

ULP!
SLAM
TRRRRRR

W-WHERE A-ARE W-WE?
I HAVE NO IDEA, BUDDY!
LET'S HAVE A LOOK!

LET'S GET THIS BOX OPEN!

WHICH PLANET IS THIS?
UH-OH!
I THINK IT'S JUST THE ATTIC, BUZZ!

ARGH! IT'S SO DARK! SO CREEPY! SO DAMP! SO SCAR-RRRY!
CALM DOWN, REX!

LET'S HAVE A LOOK!
GREAT!

SHALL WE GO WITH THEM?
YEAH! I'D LIKE TO ...

BUT YOU'VE GOT TO STEP OFF MY TAIL!
HUH?!

UHM...THE TRAPDOOR IS LOCKED!
AND THE DORMER IS SEALED...IT SEEMS WE'RE TRAPPED!

MAYBE WE CAN WAIT FOR ANDY TO COME BACK AND LOOK FOR US!
WHAT?!

WE CAN'T STAY HERE FOR THAT LONG! THERE MIGHT BE GHOSTS, MONSTERS, ZOMBIES!
COME ON, REX!

AND WHAT IF ANDY DOESN'T REMEMBER WE WERE IN THAT BOX?
REX!
WE'LL STAY HERE FOREVER!

STOP IT!!!
SORRY!

MAYBE WE CAN FIND ANOTHER WAY OUT!
GOOD IDEA, BUDDY!

I'M READY FOR A NEW MISSION!

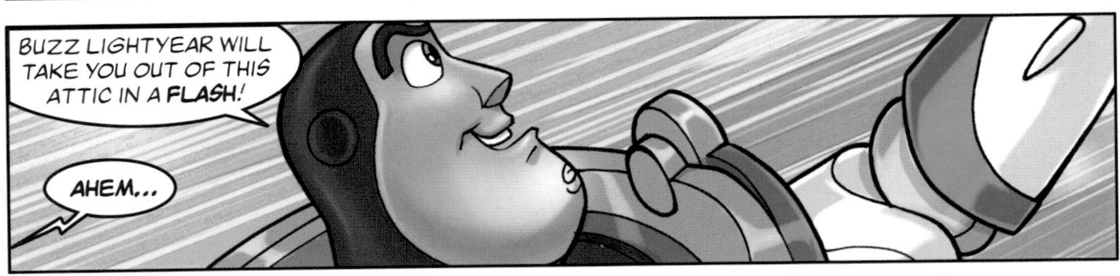
BUZZ LIGHTYEAR WILL TAKE YOU OUT OF THIS ATTIC IN A FLASH!
AHEM...

?!
IT WON'T BE SO EASY! WE NEED TO FIND A WAY TO LIGHT UP THIS PLACE FIRST!
YEAH! IT'S GETTING DARK AND WE WON'T BE ABLE TO SEE VERY WELL!

B-R-R-R! I DO-DON'T LIKE ATTICS AT NIGHT!
SHH! LET ME ANALYZE THE PROBLEM...

...YEAH! I KNOW WHAT TO DO!
SHOOTING PISTOLS!

WE'LL USE MY SUPER-**LASER**!

CLICK
EEEK!

THIS ISN'T ENOUGH TO LIGHT UP THIS PLACE, BUZZ!
BUT IT'S ENOUGH TO **BLIND** ME!

MAYBE THERE'S SOMETHING BETTER AROUND HERE!
YEAH! THIS ATTIC IS FULL OF **OLD STUFF**!

YOU CAN ALWAYS USE YOUR LASER TO SEE WHAT'S INSIDE THE BOXES!
YOU'RE RIGHT! LET'S HAVE A LOOK!

THE SEARCH FOR LIGHT BEGINS...
WE'VE GOT TO BE QUICK!
WAIT FOR ME, SLINK!
I'LL LOOK IN THOSE BOXES!
THE SHELVES ARE MINE!

LET'S SEE...

MMM...
STRAAAP

AHEM...WHY IS **STICKY TAPE** SO STICKY?!

AND WHY ISN'T THERE A **FLASHLIGHT** IN THIS BOX?!
N

IN THE MEANTIME...

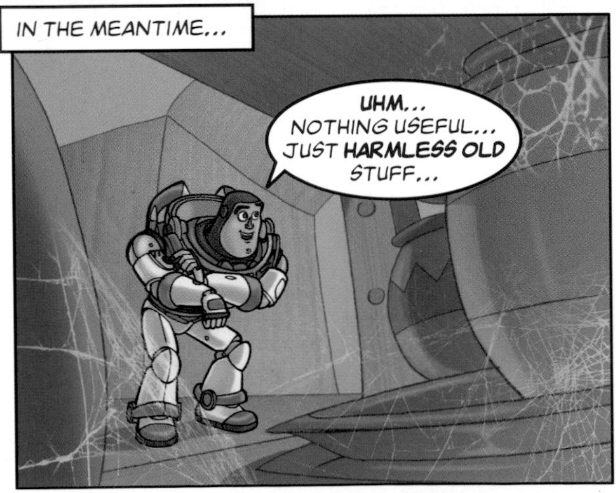

AND...

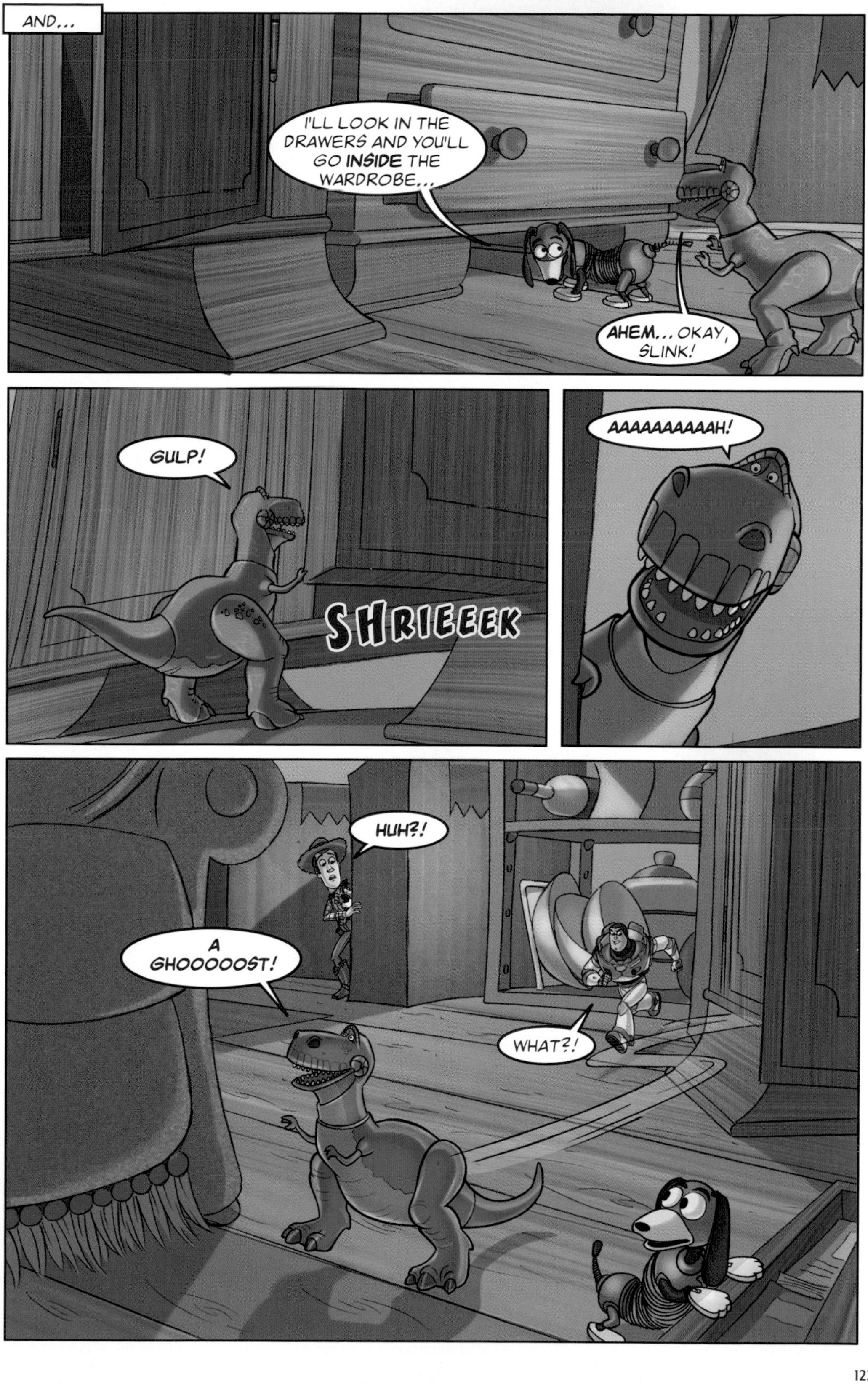

I'LL LOOK IN THE DRAWERS AND YOU'LL GO **INSIDE** THE WARDROBE...
**AHEM...** OKAY, SLINK!

GULP!
SHRIEEEK

AAAAAAAAAAH!

HUH?!

A GHOOOOOST!

WHAT?!

IT'S INSIDE THE **WA-WARDROBE**!
RELAX, REX! GHOSTS **DON'T** EXIST!

NO! I SAW IT! HE HAD A **HAT** WITH FLOWERS ON IT!
A HAT WITH **FLOWERS**?!

WELL... I SEE A **SKIRT** AND A STRAW HAT, BUT...
NO TRACES OF GHOSTS !

MAYBE **I SCARED** HIM... AFTER ALL I'M A **T-REX**!
**AHEM...**
**HEY!** LOOK UP THERE!

I THINK I'VE FOUND WHAT WE NEED!
CHRISTMAS DECORATIONS?!

YES! I REMEMBER THAT THOSE ARE BATTERY OPERATED LIGHTS!
FANTASTIC!

SLINK! DO YOU THINK YOU CAN REACH THAT BOX?

I'LL DO MY BEST, SHERIFF!
WHOA!
SPROINGGG!

POCK

HMM... THANK YOU, SLINK!
YOU COULD HAVE PLANNED A BETTER LANDING!
?!
COME ON!

AT LEAST NOW WE HAVE THE LIGHTS WE NEEDED!
BLINK

I HOPE THE BATTERIES WORK!
LET'S TRY!

CLICK

YEEES!
WE CAN SEE MUCH BETTER NOW!
!

CAN I KEEP THEM ON? THEY MAKE ME FEEL SAFE!
WELL... IF YOU WANT TO...

LET'S CHECK THE DARKEST CORNERS OF THIS DARK ATTIC!
GOOD! NOW WE CAN LOOK FOR A WAY OUT!

BUT, AFTER SOME SEARCHING...
NO! I CAN'T SEE ANY PASSAGE HERE!
IT'S USELESS!

THERE ARE NO BIG HOLES IN THE FLOOR OR IN THE WALLS!
WE CAN'T GET OUT OF HERE!
OH NO!

I SUGGEST TAKING A REST!
YEAH! NOW I'M TOO TIRED TO THINK ABOUT A PLAN B!

BUT IT'S NIGHT! I DON'T WANNA STAY HERE!
COME ON, REX! YOU HAVE YOUR LIGHTS!

SO...
COMICS! WHO WANTS TO READ WITH ME?
UHM... I DON'T FEEL LIKE READING!
DON'T WORRY, SLINK!

I'VE JUST FOUND SOMETHING TO DO!
WOW! YOU'RE THE BEST, WOODY!
TRRR

FRUSH
OKAY! LET'S PLAY!
?!

FRUSH
GULP!

HEY! I HEARD A STRANGE NOISE!
REALLY?!
NEXT WEEK
BUZZ LIGHTYEAR

IT'S A MONSTERRR!
FLAP
ARGH!
FRUSH
!
ULP!

SHHH! HE DIDN'T SEE US!
HEY! WHERE IS HE GOING?

FLAP
?!

FRUSH
A SECRET PASSAGE!

**HOORAY**! WE'RE GOING BACK TO ANDY'S ROOM!
THAT **BAT** SAVED US!
LET'S GO!

WAIT! I'LL GO FIRST AND CHECK IF THE PASSAGE IS BIG ENOUGH!
GOOD IDEA, SLINK!

POOR SLINK! HE'S NEVER STRETCHED AS MUCH AS HE HAS TODAY!
SPROINGGG

YES! WE CAN ALL GET THROUGH IT!

GREAT! BUT... HOW WILL WE GET UP THERE?
GIVE ME YOUR LIGHTS, REX!

JUST A SECOND AND...

SWISH

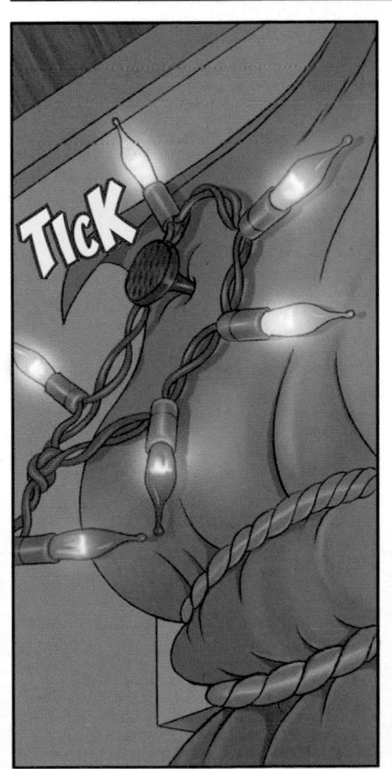
TICK

HERE YOU GO! NOW WE CAN CLIMB OUR WAY OUT MORE EASILY!
YOU'RE **GALACTIC**, BUDDY!

AND SO...
TEE, HEE!
AW! I'M TIRED!
MOVE ON, REX! PANT!

FINALLY...
I'VE CHECKED! ANDY'S WINDOW IS RIGHT BELOW HERE AND IT'S HALF OPEN!
GREAT! WE'LL GO DOWN THE WATER PIPE AND REACH IT!
PFF! THAT WAS TOUGH!

AHEM... IT SEEMS A BIT TOO SMALL FOR ME!
GO ON! YOU'LL PASS THROUGH IT WITHOUT ANY PROBLEM!

THUD
OUCH!
HEE-HEE!
ALMOST!

SWISSSS
BRRR! IT'S SO HIGH!
DON'T LOOK DOWN, REX! WE ARE NEARLY THERE!

MISSION COMPLETED!
YES! I'M STILL ALIVE!

LET'S GO IN! SOMEONE COULD SEE US!

AH! HOME SWEET HOME!
REX, WE NEVER LEFT THIS HOUSE!
WOODY!
YOU'RE BACK!

WHERE HAVE YOU BEEN?
WE THOUGHT YOU'D BEEN THROWN AWAY!
NO! IT WAS MUCH WORSE!

BUT I SAVED OUR DAY...AND OUR NIGHT TOO!
!
SHHH! ANDY'S MOM IS IN THE CORRIDOR!

I'LL GO UP TO THE ATTIC TOMORROW!
GULP!

I HEARD SOME STRANGE NOISES! THERE MIGHT BE SOME MICE!
MICE?!

PHEW! WE WERE LUCKY WE DIDN'T MEET THEM!
YES, REX! WE WERE!
POOR REX! MAYBE TOMORROW THE OTHERS WILL EXPLAIN TO HIM THAT THEY WERE THE MICE ANDY'S MOM HEARD.

THE END

# MONSTER IN THE DRAWER

TOY STORY 2

SCRIPT: TEA ORSI; PENCILS: VALENTINO FORLINI; INK: MICHELA FRARE; COLOUR: DARIO CALABRIA

BZZZZ!
BZZZ!
UH... WHAT'S THAT NOISE?!

BZZZ!
MAYBE IT'S A...

HELP! THERE'S A MONSTER IN THE DRAWER!!!
?!
UH-OH! HERE COMES MR. FRAIDY-SAURUS!

REX, THERE'S NO SUCH THING AS MONSTERS!
THEN CHECK THIS OUT!

SO...
D-DON'T YOU H-HEAR THAT AWFUL N-NOISE?!
BZZZ!
BZZZ!
HMM... SOUNDS LIKE A BUZZING MONSTER...
HOW CAN YOU TELL?!
TAKE IT EASY! I WAS JUST KIDDING!
BUT THAT SURE IS A STRANGE SOUND!
WE'D BETTER CHECK IT OUT...
BUT...
I CAN'T SEE A THING!
HOLD ON! I'LL ACTIVATE MY SPACE LASER!
ARGH!
THERE REALLY IS A MONSTER HERE!
ZZZZZ!

THIS CALLS FOR A GROUP MEETING!
NO! IT'LL CAUSE A PANIC...

...WE INTERGALACTIC HEROES WILL HAVE TO DEFEAT IT BY OURSELVES!
D-DO WE HAVE TO?!

"YEAH! PREPARE FOR ATTACK!"
READY TO STRIKE, REX?
UMM...
C'MON OUT, BUZZING MONSTER!
TRRR

DO YOU WANT WHITER TEETH?
HEY! I ALREADY HAVE A STAR-BRIGHT SMILE, YOU WISE-GUY MONSTER!
EXTRA-FRESH, THE TOOTHPASTE FOR YOU!
IT'S TELLING US TO BRUSH OUR TEETH?!?
AHEM... THIS SOUNDS SUSPICIOUS...

WOODY MAY BE ONTO SOMETHING...
YEAH, NO ONE CRITICISES MY SMILE AND GETS AWAY WITH IT!
LET'S CLIMB INTO THE DRAWER!

CHOCO CHOCK. THE CANDY BAR THAT CRUNCHES!
HMM... SOUNDS LIKE A COMMERCIAL...
YOU'RE RIGHT!

IT'S JUST ANDY'S MP3 PLAYER!
THERE'S NO MONSTER HERE!
ZZZZZ!

ANDY LEFT IT ON BY MISTAKE!
HERE'S YOUR MONSTER, REX!
?!

I HAVE TO ADMIT I WAS ALMOST SCARED!
SSH... DON'T LET WORD GET ROUND! HA, HA!

THE END

# AN AFTERNOON WITH ZURG

SCRIPT: SIMONA GRANDI; PENCILS: LUCA USAI; INK: MICHELA FRARE; COLOUR: GIANLUCA BARONE

WHILE ANDY GOES DOWNSTAIRS, THE TOYS KEEP PLAYING...
OKAY, GUYS, HERE'S THE PLAN!

WE'LL ATTACK ZURG BY SURPRISE!

WHILE I PROVIDE A DIVERSION...

...I'LL SURROUND HIM WITH MY SPRING!

GET SET, THE ENEMY'S APPROACHING!

AT THAT VERY MOMENT...
SEE, REX...

YOU'VE GOT TO LEARN TO WALK LIKE A REAL SPACE EMPEROR!
HOW'S THIS?
WOW! YOU'RE GREAT, REX!
THANKS, BUZZ. YOU'VE BEEN A BIG HELP!
WHAT ARE FRIENDS FOR? NOW SHOW ME A SUPER SPACE SPIN!
SOMEBODY IS WAITING IN AMBUSH.
READY FOR ACTION!

WATCH THIS AWESOME INTERGALACTIC MOVE!
BUT WITH ONE FLICK OF THE TAIL...
SWISHHH!
BAMMM!
YOU WON!
NICE GOING, REX! YOU'RE A TRUE SPACE PREDATOR!
A SURPRISE MOVE WORTHY OF EMPEROR ZURG!
ZURG? HERE? YIKES!
THE NEXT SPACE MISSION WON'T BE FOR A LONG TIME...
THE END

Disney · PIXAR
TOY STORY 2

# SPACE STATION HIGH JINKS

ANDY HAD BEEN DREAMING OF THIS MOMENT FOR A LONG TIME, AND AT LAST...
THANKS, MOM! THIS IS THE **COOLEST** PRESENT I'VE EVER GOTTEN!
...THE **SPACE RANGERS STATION** IS HIS!
CODE-1 ALARM, BUZZ! ASTRO-TICKS ON THE ATTACK!
NO PROBLEM, WOODY! THEY'RE NO MATCH FOR THE NEW TURBO-POWERED SPACE STATION!
ANDY'S NEVER HAD THIS MUCH FUN!
AND NEITHER HAS BUZZ!

SCRIPT: ALESSANDRO FERRARI; PENCILS: VALENTINO FORLINI; INK: MICHELA FRARE; PAINT: MARA DAMIANI.

THE NEXT MORNING, WHILE ANDY'S AT SCHOOL...
HERE SHE IS! WHAT DO YOU SAY?
OUT OF THIS WORLD!
WOW!
IT'LL DO...

IT'LL DO? HEY, IT'S LOADED WITH LASER CANNONS!
AND A TELETRANSPORT PLATFORM!
AND TURBO-POWERED EMERGENCY CAPSULES!

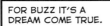

FOR BUZZ IT'S A DREAM COME TRUE.

THAT'S **WAY BEYOND** IT'LL DO!

A DREAM HE WANTS TO SHARE WITH HIS FRIENDS...
LOOK, IT'S BIG ENOUGH FOR ALL OF US!
YOU MEAN WE CAN...
OF COURSE! IT'S **YOUR** SPACE STATION **TOO**, MY FRIEND! FROM NOW ON...

...YOU ALL ARE HONORARY SPACE RANGE... HEY, WHERE ARE YOU GOING?!
ZWOOM

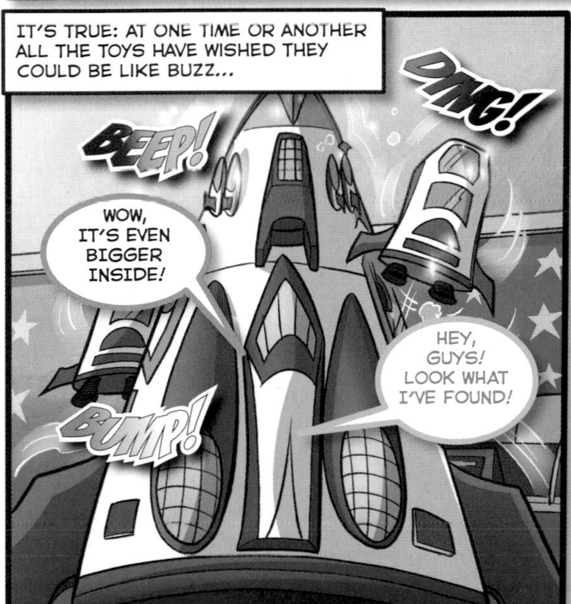
IT'S TRUE: AT ONE TIME OR ANOTHER ALL THE TOYS HAVE WISHED THEY COULD BE LIKE BUZZ...
DING!
BEEP!
WOW, IT'S EVEN BIGGER INSIDE!
HEY, GUYS! LOOK WHAT I'VE FOUND!
BUMP!

...AND HERE'S THEIR CHANCE!
ARE YOU THINKING WHAT I'M THINKING?

THROOP
CLINK
RIP

REX LIGHTYEAR TO THE RESCUE!

DOG COMMAND, DO YOU READ ME? OVER.

LASER ACTIVATED!

OH, NO!

TO INFINITY AND BEYOND!

FOR BUZZ, MAYBE THE SPACE STATION WASN'T SUCH A GREAT GIFT AFTER ALL!

THE END

DISNEP · PIXAR
TOY STORY 2

# SCARY TALE

IT'S LATE IN ANDY'S ROOM AND HIS TOYS ARE LISTENING TO A HORROR STORY READ BY HAMM...
I WAS IN MY LABORATORY ONE DARK, STORMY NIGHT, THINKING OVER MY CREEPY EXPERIMENTS...

...WHEN I NOTICED THE RADIOACTIVE MONSTER'S CAGE WAS OPEN...

...AND THE TOY-EATING CREATURE HAD DISAPPEARED!

HEY, YOU!

AAAH! THE RADIOACTIVE MONSTER! EVERY TOY FOR HIMSELF!

BLAST IT, REX! YOU FRIGHTENED AWAY MY AUDIENCE BEFORE I FINISHED THE STORY!
ERR, SORRY HAMM... I THOUGHT YOU SAID THE WORD! CAN WE TRY AGAIN?

THE END

SCRIPT: ALESSANDRO FERRARI; PENCILS: VALENTINO FORLINI; INKS: MICHELA FRARE; PAINT: MARA DAMIANI.

TOY STORY 3

# LASSO BOOMERANG

SCRIPT: ALESSANDRO SISTI; LAYOUT & INK: LUCA USAI; COLOUR: MARA DAMIANI & LUCIO DE GIUSEPPE

# LET'S GO TO THE MOVIES

ANDY'S WATCHING A WESTERN ON TV...

YEE-HAA! RIDE, COWBOY!

SCRIPT: CARLO PANARO; PENCILS: LUCA USAI; INK: MICHELA FRARE; COLOUR: KAWAII CREATIVE STUDIO

THAT WAS REALLY SOME MOVIE!
I WONDER HOW IT ENDS.

LET'S TURN IT BACK ON!

THE END
OH, NO! WE'VE MISSED IT!
WHAT A SHAME!

DON'T WORRY! I KNOW HOW IT ENDS--I'VE SEEN IT BEFORE!
TELL US WHAT HAPPENS, WOODY!

I'LL DO BETTER THAN THAT! I'LL **ACT IT OUT** FOR YOU!

WOODY PRETENDS TO BE THE COWBOY IN THE FILM...
THIS IS WHAT HAPPENS NEXT, GUYS! WATCH CAREFULLY.
GREAT ACTING, WOODY!
IT'S JUST LIKE WATCHING TV!
BUT THEN THINGS START TO GO WRONG...
AAAH!
SWIIISH!
BAMM
IS THAT WHAT HAPPENS IN THE FILM?
ERR... SURE!
AND AFTER THAT THE BRAVE COWBOY FREES THE BEAUTIFUL GIRL!

AND THEY RIDE OFF INTO THE SUNSET...

SUDDENLY, THE SADDLE SLIPS!
OUCH!
THUD!

ERR.. THAT WASN'T QUITE WHAT HAPPENED IN THE FILM...
HMMM!

...BUT IT GIVES YOU AN IDEA OF HOW THE STORY ENDS!
GEE, MORE OR LESS!

HA! HA! HA!
I THOUGHT IT WAS A WESTERN, NOT A COMEDY!
THE END

# SNACK CLUB

SCRIPT: ALESSANDRO SISTI; LAYOUT: ANDREA GREPPI; INK: MICHELA FRARE; COLOUR: ANGELA CAPOLUPO

I'M READY TO GO HOME, MUM!

WAIT A MOMENT, DARLING! THE SNACKS VENDING MACHINE HAS BEEN BROKEN FOR A WHILE!

OUT OF ORDER

I SENT FOR THE TECHNICIAN, HE SAID HE WOULD COME TODAY!

HE SHOULD BE HERE ANY MINUTE! COME ON, BONNIE, LET'S GO AND WAIT FOR HIM!

OH, NO! WHAT A MESS!

THE TECHNICIAN COULD DISCOVER OUR CLUB WHEN HE REPAIRS THE VENDING MACHINE!
WE HAVE TO REMOVE THE FURNISHINGS!

STRETCH! CHUNK! YOU'RE IN CHARGE OF MOVING STUFF...

... AND I'LL GUARD AND WARN YOU IF ANYONE ARRIVES!

BUT SOON...
UH-OH! **ALARM!**
GROAN! WE HAD JUST STARTED!
Snacks!
THE TECHNICIAN'S ARRIVED!

WE HAVE TO HIDE!
LET'S TAKE COVER UNDER THE SNACKS!
YOU SEE? THE MACHINE SEEMS BROKEN!
LET'S HAVE A LOOK AT THE BACK!
Snacks!
JUST A BROKEN SWITCH, IT'S AN EASY FIX!
NOW IT'S WORKING PROPERLY! LET'S TEST IT!
BEEP-BEEP
OUT OF ORDER

GULP! WHAT'S UP?

ZZZZZZZZZZZZ

CLONK CLONK

UH?

WHAT A STRANGE SOUND!

OOH! LOOK!

# THE LITTLE LIGHTNING

IT'S RAINING CATS AND DOGS!
THE PERFECT EVENING TO MEET YOUR FRIENDS!

IT'S A PITY THAT SPARKY DIDN'T COME!
YAWN! IT'S LATE! LET'S GO TO SLEEP!

TOMORROW WILL BE A DAY WITH PLENTY OF PLAYING!
YOU'RE RIGHT, STRETCH! WE HAVE TO BE IN GOOD SHAPE TO...


SCRIPT: ALESSANDRO SISTI; LAYOUT & INK: VALENTINO FORLINO; COLOUR: LUCIO DE GIUSEPPE

UH? WHAT'S UP?!
OH, NO! A BLACKOUT!

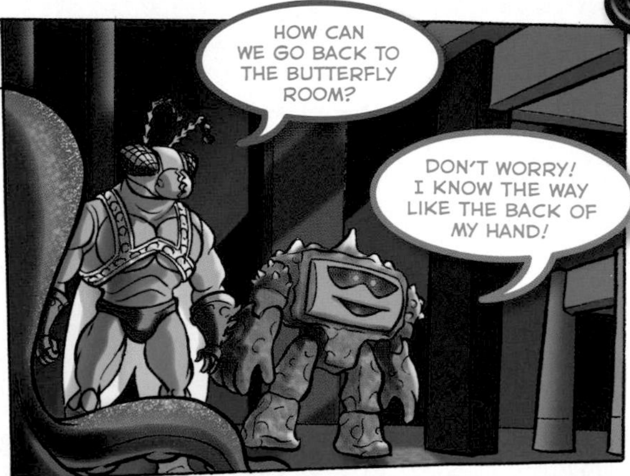
HOW CAN WE GO BACK TO THE BUTTERFLY ROOM?
DON'T WORRY! I KNOW THE WAY LIKE THE BACK OF MY HAND!

WE WILL BE BACK HOME IN A JIFFY... OUCH!
BONK!

GRUNT! I DIDN'T SEE IT!
OBVIOUSLY! IT'S PITCH DARK!

BAROOOM
LUCKILY YOU HAVE A HARD HEAD!
K-RAAK
BUT IT HURTS ALL THE SAME!
AAARGH!

WHAT'S THE MATTER WITH YOU, TWITCH?
THUNDER AND LIGHTNING SCARES ME!
IF LIGHTNING STRUCK US, WE WOULD TURN INTO MELTED PLASTIC!
CALM DOWN! THAT'S IMPOSSIBLE!
SUNNYSIDE IS SAFE! NO LIGHTNING COULD GET IN HERE!
PERHAPS A LITTLE LIGHTNING COULD ... ?
... LIKE THE ONE THAT IS COMING THERE!
SFRRRCHT
SFRZZZ
LET'S HIDE!
IT REALLY IS A LIGHTNING!
AND IT'S COMING TOWARDS US!

I CAN SEE ITS EYES! IT IS...

... SPARKY?
HI, MY FRIENDS!

WHAT ARE YOU DOING HERE?
I REALIZED YOU WEREN'T COMING BACK AND CAME TO YOUR RESCUE!

AND I BROUGHT A TORCH!
THANK YOU! WE REALLY NEED IT!
CLICK
WHY DIDN'T YOU SWITCH ON YOUR TORCH FROM THE BEGINNING?
A ROBOT WITH A PERSONAL RESERVE OF LIGHTNING DOESN'T NEED IT!

THE END

# ANSWER IN THE BOOKS

DISNEY · PIXAR TOY STORY 3

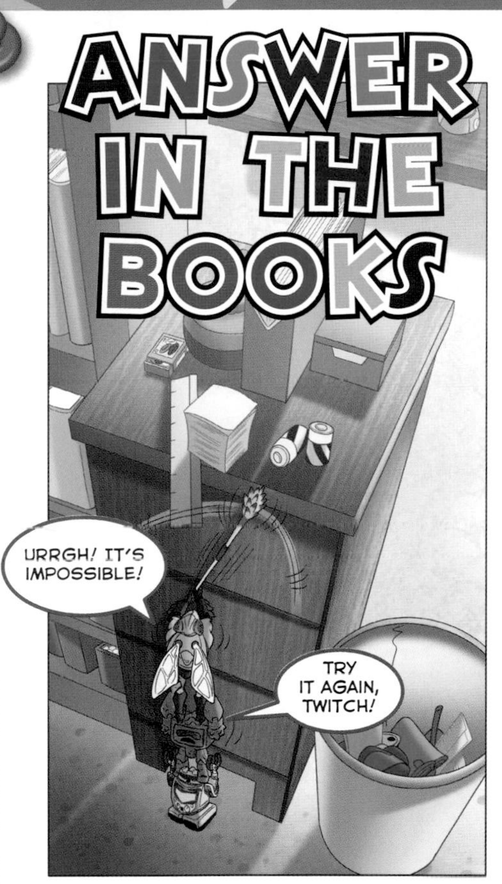

URRGH! IT'S IMPOSSIBLE!
TRY IT AGAIN, TWITCH!

SPARKS NEEDS THOSE BATTERIES!
I'VE GOT AN IDEA!

I TIE THIS STRING TO MY STICK...

... AND THROW IT!
SWIISH

SO WE CAN USE IT TO CLIMB!
GULP! LOOK OUT!

BONK
THUD
OUCH! THAT WASN'T A GOOD IDEA!
BETTER ASK BOOKWORM FOR ADVICE! HE KNOWS EVERYTHING!

SCRIPT: ALESSANDRO SISTI, PENCILS & INKS: VALENTINO FORLINI, COLOR: ANGELA CAPOLUPO

BUT...
I'M SORRY! I CAN'T FIND A SOLUTION!

I SUGGEST YOU SEARCH FOR IT IN THE BOOKS!
UHM... OK...

YOU ALWAYS FIND WHAT YOU NEED IN BOOKS!

A LITTLE LATER...
THANK YOU, BOOKWORM! YOU WERE RIGHT!

THE ANSWER WAS IN BOOKS!
HA! HA! NOT EXACTLY WHAT I MEANT... BUT IT WORKED!
THE END

# TWITCH SEES EVERYTHING

SCRIPT: ALESSANDRO SISTI; LAYOUT: GIANFRANCO FLORIO; INK: MICHELA FRARE; COLOUR: ANGELA CAPOLUPO

I HAVE A SECRET! MY INSECT EYES CAN SEE EVERYTHING...
...EVEN THROUGH THE WALLS!
TEE-HEE! I DON'T BELIEVE YOU!
NOR DO I! PROVE IT!
I HAVE AN IDEA! TWITCH GOES OUT OF THE ROOM AND THEN WE DO SOMETHING!
THEN HE COMES BACK AND SAYS WHAT WE DID DURING HIS ABSENCE!
OK!
TWITCH WILL NEVER GUESS IT!
LET ME CALL HIM!

BUT...
BARBIE AND KEN CLIMBED ON TOP OF CHUNK!
OOH!
HE REALLY SAW US!
I TOLD YOU! LET'S DO IT AGAIN, SO YOU ARE CONVINCED!
THIS TIME WE COULD...
WAIT! I THINK TWITCH HAS TRICKED US!
I WANT TO SEE WHAT HE'S DOING! LET'S FOLLOW HIM SECRETLY!
AND...
LOOK! HE IS GOING INTO THE CONTROL ROOM!

TWITCH'S EYES DON'T HAVE ANYTHING SPECIAL! HE SAW US FROM THE MONITOR!
THAT IS EXACTLY WHAT HAPPENED! YOU GOT ME!
THAT WAS A REALLY A GOOD TRICK... AND IT GIVES ME A GREAT IDEA FOR A NEW GAME!
A LITTLE LATER...
LOOK AT ME!
HA! HA! THEY ARE FUNNY!
PLAYING TV SHOWS IS MORE FUN THAN HIDE-AND-SEEK!
NOW IT'S OUR TURN!
THE END

# SIMPLY... TENTACULAR

BUT...
UGG! IT'S TOO HEAVY!
CAN YOU LEND A... TENTACLE, STRETCH?
SURE!
HUH?
VRAAM
HOORAY!
THANKS! YOU'RE REALLY STRONG!
WHAT'S THE MATTER WITH HER? I PAID HER A COMPLIMENT, BUT SHE DOESN'T LOOK TOO HAPPY!
SIGH!
YOU FORGET THAT STRETCH IS A GIRL, CHUNK!

OH! I SEE...
AND SOMETIMES SHE LIKES TO BE TREATED LIKE ONE!
BUT IT'S NOT MY FAULT! SHE DOESN'T LOOK MUCH LIKE A GIRL!
HMM!
CHUNK'S RIGHT! SHE NEEDS HELP WITH HER LOOK!
AND I KNOW JUST THE THING! BARBIE, CAN I BORROW A FEW ITEMS?
NO PROBLEM! WHAT DO YOU NEED?
SOON...
HEY, EVERYBODY! GATHER AROUND!

TWITCH IS CALLING US. LET'S GO SEE!
IS SOMETHING THE MATTER?
NO, EVERYTHING'S FINE! I JUST WANT TO INTRODUCE YOU TO...
...STRETCH AND HER NEW LOOK!
MY CLOTHES MAKE THE DIFFERENCE!
SHEER ELEGANCE, EH?
ONLY STRETCH COULD WEAR FOUR DIFFERENT OUTFITS AT THE SAME TIME! HA! HA!
THE END

# LET'S STRETCH!

SUNNYSIDE DAYCARE, ON A BRIGHT AND CHEERY DAY...
HA! HA! HA!
STRETCH IS HARD AT WORK...

...AS SHE'S SUNNYSIDE'S MOST FUN-LOVING TOY!
INCREDIBLE! HEY, CHUNK, HER JOKES MUST BE REALLY FUNNY...
HA! HA! HA!

NO, USUALLY HER JOKES ARE A BIT SILLY...
TEE-HEE-HEE!

HA! HA! HA!

TEE-HEE-HEE!

!!!
...BUT WHO CAN RESIST ALL THOSE **TICKLING TENTACLES?**
THE END

SCRIPT: ALESSANDRO FERRARI; PENCILS: VALENTINO FORLINI; INK: FEDERICA SALFO; PAINT: GIANLUCA BARONE

# LOW-FLYING TOYS!

REX, THE NEXT TIME YOU THINK OF TELLING BUZZ THERE'S ANOTHER TOY HERE AT **SUNNYSIDE** THAT HAS WINGS...

WHOOM!
...DON'T DO IT, OKAY?!
SORRY, JESSIE! I DIDN'T THINK BUZZ AND TWITCH WOULD START A FLYING CONTEST...
NOT BAD, BUZZ, BUT I CAN DO BETTER...

MOMENTS LATER, TWITCH FLEW PAST, PASSING DANGEROUSLY CLOSE TO THE TOYS ON THE GROUND!
WHOOOOM!
YEAHHH!

I WON THE FLYING CONTEST, SPACE RANGER!
NOT SO FAST, INSECT-MAN! IT'S TIME TO SEE WHO CAN FLY THE **LOWEST** IN OUR NEXT CONTEST WE'LL CALL... **GROUND-GRAZING!**

G-G-GROUND-GRAZING?
OH NO! NOW WE'RE REALLY IN FOR IT!

THE END

SCRIPT: ALESSANDRO FERRARI; PENCILS: ETTORE GULA; INK: MICHELA FRARE; PAINT: MARA DAMIANI

Disney · PIXAR
TOY STORY 3
SOLDIER'S SECRET
IT'S RECESS TIME AT SUNNYSIDE. THE KIDS ARE HAVING A PICNIC OUTSIDE...
...AND THE TOYS HAVE A GUEST: TODAY BONNIE BROUGHT BUZZ!
EVERY TIME I SEE YOU, I REMEMBER THE RESCUES IN ANDY'S ROOM, SARGE!
YES! THOSE WERE REALLY TOUGH MISSIONS!
WHAT ARE YOU TALKING ABOUT?
IT WAS A GAME WE USED TO PLAY WITH ANDY!
OH! I DON'T REMEMBER!
WHAT DID YOU DO?
UHM... THE FOUR OF US ARE NOT ENOUGH TO SHOW YOU!
YES! WE NEED MORE SOLDIERS!
WE COULD DO IT TOGETHER! IT'LL BE FUN!
YES!
COOL! JUST LET ME CHANGE MY OUTFIT!

SCRIPT: TEA ORSI; ROUGH LAYOUT: LUCIO LEONI;
CLEAN LAYOUT: LUCA USAI; COLOUR: ANGELA CAPOLUPO

SHORTLY AFTER...
OKAY, SOLDIERS! NOW WE NEED SOMEONE TO RESCUE!
ME, ME! I'VE NEVER BEEN RESCUED!
GOOD! NOW YOU HAVE TO CLIMB ON TOP OF THE DREAM HOUSE!
BUT IT'S TOO DANGEROUS FOR A SWEET GIRL!
DON'T WORRY, KEN! I'LL TAKE THE ELEVATOR!
IN FACT...
AND...
I'M READY!
WE CAN START THE RESCUE OPERATIONS!
YEAH! WE'LL REACH BARBIE AND TAKE HER BACK TO THE FLOOR!
BUT REMEMBER! THE SOLDIER'S SECRET IS--
I WANNA GO FIRST!

I'LL REACH YOU IN A JIFFY, BARBIE!
LET'S SEE!
SIGH!

BUT...
OH NO! I'M SLIPPING!

BIG BABY'S IDEA IS NOT GOOD EITHER...
OOOH!
TRRRR TRRR
ARGH! MY POOR HOUSE!

AND THEN IT'S KEN'S TURN...
C'MON BARBIE! JUST A LITTLE TINY EFFORT!
HEY! THIS DOESN'T LOOK LIKE A RESCUE!

COME DOWN AND LET ME EXPLAIN!

FINALLY
THE SOLDIER'S SECRET IS **TEAMWORK!**
YEAH! WE SHOULD JOIN OUR FORCES TO COMPLETE THE MISSION!
**HUH?!** YOU'RE RIGHT!
COOL, BUT... HOW WILL WE RESCUE BARBIE?
IT'S EASY! WE'LL MAKE A **TOY TOWER** AND HELP HER GET BACK TO THE ELEVATOR!
THE TOYS CLIMB ON EACH OTHER SHOULDERS AND...
YOU ARE SAFE, BEAUTIFUL BARBIE!
MISSION ACCOMPLISHED!
HEY! HOLD ON A MINUTE!
HOW WILL WE GET BACK DOWN NOW?
AHEM... THAT'S ANOTHER SOLDIER'S SECRET! **HEE, HEE!**
THE END

# BOOT CAMP?

Disney · PIXAR
TOY STORY 3

OKAY FOLKS, ARE YOU READY FOR THE TRAINING?
WHAT KIND OF TRAINING, SARGE?

WE'VE ORGANIZED A BOOT CAMP!
BOOT CAMP?!

DON'T WORRY, BUDDY! IT'S NOTHING DANGEROUS, JUST A BIT OF EXERCISE.
I KNOW, BUT I NEED SOMETHING BEFORE WE CAN START.

I'LL BE RIGHT BACK!
?

AND...
I CAN'T TAKE PART IN A BOOT CAMP WITHOUT A FANCY PAIR OF BOOTS!
!


THE END

SCRIPT: TEA ORSI, PENCILS: LUCA USAI, INKS: MICHELA FRARE, COLOR: ANGELA CAPOLUPO

# THE BEST REMEDY

SCRIPT: TEA ORSI; LAYOUT & INK: LUCA USAI; COLOUR: MARA DAMIANI

Disney · PIXAR TOY STORY 3

# A DAY OF REST

SCRIPT: TEA ORSI; PENCILS&INK: VALENTINO FORLINI; COLOUR: MARA DAMIANI

ONE EVENING...
I'M A WRECK!
YOU SAID IT! WE COULD USE SOME REST!

WE USED TO GET LOTS OF REST!
ARE YOU SERIOUS?!

I SURE AM! THE SECRET TO PEACE AND QUIET FOR US TOYS CAN BE FOUND IN THAT OLD ALBUM!
LET'S TAKE A LOOK! QUICK!
HUH!

HERE WE ARE! PANT!

THERE WEREN'T MANY OF US BACK THEN, SO THE KIDS PLAYED WITH WATER AND FLOUR...
WOW!

AND NEWSPAPERS!

AND PASTA!
LOOKS LIKE FUN!

HMM... WHAT IF...?

LET'S GO, SLINK! I'VE GOT AN IDEA!
?!

SOON...
ALL WE NEED IS RIGHT HERE!
BETTER THAN A TOY STORE! HEE-HEE!

WOODY'S GOT A PLAN...
FLOUR COMIN' AT YOU!
WATCH IT...!

COUGH! COUGH!

FLYING PASTA!
NICE SHOT!

LATER ON...
WE'LL LEAVE IT ALL HERE... AND HOPE IT WORKS!

THE NEXT MORNING...
HEY! WHERE'D ALL THIS STUFF COME FROM?!
THIS IS IT!

WELL... MAYBE IT'S NOT SUCH A BAD IDEA AFTER ALL!
KIDS! TODAY WE'RE GOING TO PLAY A NEW GAME!
YES!

WHAT'S GOIN' ON?!
NOW THAT THE KIDS ARE OCCUPIED, WE CAN GET THAT DAY OF REST WE NEEDED!
AH-HA...GOOD THINKING, WOODY!
THE END

# DRASTIC CURE

SCRIPT: ALESSANDRO SISTI; PENCILS: LUCA USAI; INK: MICHELA FRARE; COLOUR: GIANLUCA BARONE

BOOKWORM CHECKS CHUNK'S MANUAL...
SORRY, THIS DOESN'T TELL ME ANYTHING.
BUT A WHACK ON THE HEAD MIGHT HELP.
LET'S TRY IT. TWITCH?
WHACK!
I'M NOT STRONG ENOUGH!
COOL IT! I HAVE AN IDEA!
THIS WAY, CHUNK.
OK, BUT NO MORE TICKLING!
AND NO JOKES!
NO, WE JUST WANT TO TAKE YOU...

...IN HERE!
HUH?
HOLD HIM, STRETCH! THE KIDS WILL BE COMING SOON!
ARGH! NOT THE CATERPILLAR ROOM!
NO!
OPEN UP!
JUST THEN...
LOOK AT THAT TOY!
IT LOOKS LIKE A STONE!
I NEED A STONE.

WE CAN HIT WITH IT!
LET ME TRY!
THUD!
BOMP!
POOR CHUNK!
WHAT HAVE WE DONE?
IT'S TOO LATE TO HELP!
BREAKTIME FINALLY ARRIVES...
COME ON, LET'S GET CHUNK BACK!
YEAH! IT WORKED!
HE'S NOT STUCK ANY MORE!
ARE YOU ANGRY WITH US, CHUNK?
SORRY, WE JUST WANTED TO HELP.
NO, I CAN'T BE ANGRY.
BECAUSE NOW... I'M STUCK ON HAPPY!
THE END

# DRESSED TO THRILL

IT'S SUNDAY AND KEN IS HAVING A PARTY...
HEY, EVERYTHING LOOKS GREAT!
REALLY COOL, KEN!
OKAY, GUYS, SAVE YOUR COMPLI-MENTS FOR TONIGHT!

HERE ARE YOUR MAGICAL INVITATIONS!
YOU'RE NOT FOOLIN' AROUND, KEN!

UMM...

WHAT DOES DRESSED TO THRILL MEAN?
THAT'S EASY, MY DEAR SHERIFF!
GUESTS MUST COME DRESSED TO THRILL

SCRIPT: ALESSANDRO SISTI; PENCILS: GIANLUCA BARONE; INK: MICHELA FRARE; COLOUR: KAWAII CREATIVE STUDIO

IT MEANS YOU CAN'T COME TO THE PARTY WEARING YOUR OLD COWBOY OUTFITS!
?!

AND THOSE SPACE SUITS ARE DEFINITELY OUT OF STYLE!
OOOH!

OF COURSE, MY SPACE RANGER UNIFORM WILL BE FINE FOR YOUR PARTY, RIGHT, PAL?
GEE... ACTUALLY...

IT'S NOT EXACTLY IN KEEPING WITH THE PARTY'S THEME, BUZZ!
WHAT?!

YOU'VE GOT TO BE ELEGANT, STYLISH AND CHIC... IN SHORT... YOU'VE GOT TO DRESS LIKE ME!
IS HE SERIOUS?
I'M AFRAID SO!

ONCE KEN HAS LEFT...
NOW WHAT?
I DON'T HAVE ANY OTHER CLOTHES!
DON'T WORRY... FOLLOW ME!

WE'LL FIND EVERYTHING WE NEED...
CLACK

...RIGHT HERE INSIDE KEN'S DREAM HOUSE!
WOW! LOOK AT ALL THESE CLOTHES!

ARE YOU SURE KEN WON'T GET MAD?
WELL... HE'S THE ONE WHO ASKED US TO CHANGE...

THEN HE'S IN FOR A SURPRISE ALRIGHT!
YIPPEE!

THAT EVENING...
SURPRISE!
HUH?!

HEY... THOSE ARE MY ABSOLUTELY PRECIOUS CLOTHES YOU'RE WEARING!
RIGHT YOU ARE!
YOU SAID YOU WANTED US TO DRESS LIKE YOU!

AND WE'VE DONE JUST THAT!
I GUESS YOU HAVE! SIGH!
A LITTLE WHILE LATER...
WATCH IT! YOU'LL RUIN MY SCARVES!
POOR KEN! HE SURE IS PROTECTIVE OF HIS CLOTHES!
LOOKS LIKE HE'LL HAVE TO COME UP WITH A NEW THEME FOR HIS NEXT PARTY! HA! HA!
THE END

Disney · PIXAR
TOY STORY 3

# A SANDY ADVENTURE

ONE AFTERNOON IN THE CATERPILLAR ROOM...
OKAY, EVERYBODY OUTSIDE!
SWISSSH

LATER ON...
RIIING!
THE CHILDREN HAVE GONE HOME!

BULLSEYE'S BEEN LEFT ON THE PLAYGROUND ALL BY HIMSELF!
POOR DEAR!
DON'T PANIC, LADIES!

BUZZ LIGHTYEAR WILL SAVE HIM!
I'M COMING WITH YOU!

A LITTLE WHILE LATER...
OUCH!
HOW MUCH FURTHER?
WE DID IT!
THUMP
PANT! WASN'T THERE AN EASIER WAY OUT?
OR ONE WITH NO TENTACLES IN THE WAY?
GREAT! NOW LET'S FIND BULLSEYE!
I THINK I'VE ALREADY FOUND HIM!
HE MUST BE INSIDE! LET'S GO!
HEE
PRRR
THUMP THUMP
HEY, HORSEY!!!
HUH!?
LOOKS LIKE HE'S HAVING FUN!
THUMP THUMP

BUT HE CAN'T GET OUT!
DON'T WORRY! I HAVE A PLAN!

WE'LL MAKE A CHAIN!
YESSIR!
?!

ARGH! I CAN'T HOLD ON!
JUST A LITTLE MORE!

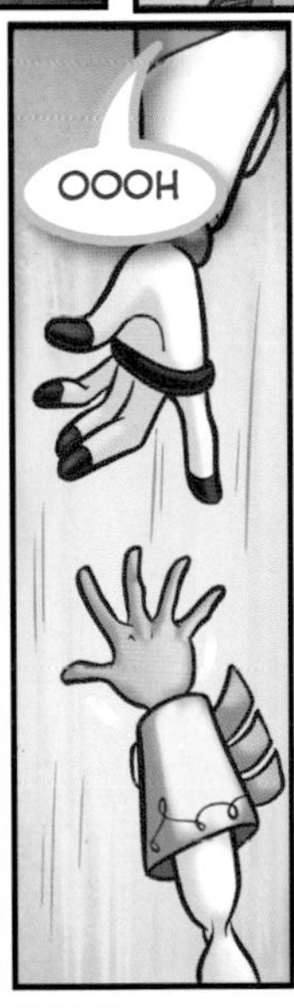
OOOH

HELP!
THUMP
!?

DRAT! WE NEED A NEW SUPERGALACTIC PLAN!
SIGH!

THAT'S IT! I'LL GET A ROPE, LOWER MYSELF INSIDE THE SANDPIT, AND BLAH, BLAH... ARE YOU GETTING ALL THIS, STRETCH?!
STRE... WHAT THE...?!
WE'RE ALMOST THERE, GUYS!
WOW!
GREAT JOB, STRETCH!
TIC
ERRT
SWISH
TIC
WOW, STRETCH... YOU DID GREAT!
SOMETIMES HAVING LOTS OF TENTACLES IS BETTER THAN ONE SUPERGALACTIC PLAN. HEE, HEE!
THE END

Disney · Pixar Toy Story 3

# GARDEN GUARDIANS

LET'S GO, BONNIE!

I'M COMING, MUM!

SIGH! I'VE FORGOTTEN WOODY AT THE SUNNYSIDE!

IT'S LATE! GRANDMA IS EXPECTING US FOR DINNER!

SCRIPT: ALESSANDRO SISTI; LAYOUT & INK: VALENTINO FORLINI; COLOUR: LUCIO DE GIUSEPPE

IT WILL BE LIKE A LITTLE HOLIDAY IN THE NURSERY! I'LL GO INTO THE GARDEN TO TAKE A WALK!

UH?

HEY! IS THERE ANYBODY THERE?

COME OUT, MY FRIEND! DON'T...

TWOOING
GASP!

OOOH!
STOP IT! HANDS UP!

IN THE MEANTIME...
WHERE'S WOODY?
THE SHERIFF IS IN THE GARDEN!

WHAT? DIDN'T YOU WARN HIM THAT THEY ARE THERE?

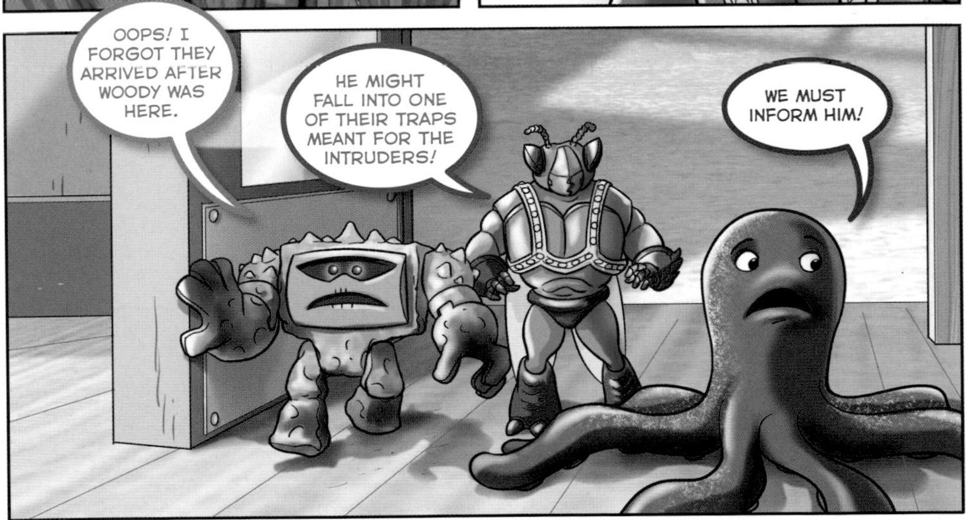
OOPS! I FORGOT THEY ARRIVED AFTER WOODY WAS HERE.
HE MIGHT FALL INTO ONE OF THEIR TRAPS MEANT FOR THE INTRUDERS!
WE MUST INFORM HIM!

WE GOT WORRIED FOR NOTHING!
IT SEEMS THEY KNOW EACH OTHER!
LUCKILY THEY DIDN'T SEE ME HANGING BY THE TRAP!
IT WAS A PLEASURE TO MEET YOU AGAIN, SIR!
THE END

# SUNNYSIDE DANCE CONTEST

SCRIPT: TEA ORSI; LAYOUT: ANDREA GREPPI; INK: MICHELA FRARE; COLOUR: LUCIO DE GIUSEPPE

THERE'S A DANCE CONTEST AT THE DAYCARE TOMORROW...
OOH! I LOVE BALLET!
SHHH! LET HER SPEAK!

"EVERYONE WANTS TO COMPETE..."
I COULD WIN IN MY DISCO OUTFIT!
YEAH! WHAT FUN!

...EXCEPT ME!
SO YOU CAME BACK HERE TO AVOID THE CONTEST?

I HAD TO! I HAVE LOTS OF ARMS BUT NO LEGS! I CAN'T DANCE!
WELL, YOU CAN'T GIVE UP!
YEAH! WE'LL HELP YOU!

YOU'LL DO THAT? REALLY?
YES...I JUST HAVE TO COME UP WITH A PLAN!
YOU DON'T NEED A PLAN! YOU NEED A DANCE TEACHER!

START WITH A PLIÉ, A PASSÉ, AND A PIROUETTE!
PLI..WHAT?!
DON'T ASK ME!

SORRY! IT'S TOO DIFFICULT!
EVEN WE DON'T UNDERSTAND WHAT YOU SAY!
WELL... MAYBE YOU'RE RIGHT...

LET'S MAKE STRETCH USE HER ARMS!
INTERESTING! ALTERNATIVE DANCE!

THE FIRST ATTEMPT IS NOT PERFECT...
SOMEONE UNTANGLE ME, PLEASE!
OH DEAR! WHAT A MESS!

BUT THEN...
NOT BAD! AND LET ME SUGGEST A SPECIAL MOVE FOR YOU!
WHAT IF YOU ALSO... PSST... PSST...
WOW! I DIDN'T KNOW YOU WERE A DANCE EXPERT, HAMM!
AMAZING! BRAVO!
CLAP
CLAP
CLAP

NEXT NIGHT, AT SUNNYSIDE...
THIS IS SO COOL!
YEAH!
KEEP SPINNING!

WHERE DID YOU LEARN TO DANCE LIKE THAT?
IT'S A SECRET! TEE-HEE!
HEY! BARBIE'S ANNOUNCING THE WINNER...

AND THE WINNER IS... **STRETCH!**
ME? ARE YOU SERIOUS?
IT'S INCREDIBLE, BUT... YOU WERE EVEN BETTER THAN ME!
CLAP
CLAP
CLAP

THANK YOU! I DEDICATE THIS PRIZE TO SOME VERY SPECIAL FRIENDS!
YES, STRETCH! SOMETIMES GOOD FRIENDS CAN MAKE YOU FEEL LIKE A REAL STAR!
THE END

# A SUNNYSIDE WEEKEND

BONNIE LEFT DOLLY AND MR. PRICKLEPANTS AT SUNNYSIDE FOR THE WEEKEND...
WHY OH WHY DID SHE LEAVE US IN THIS MESSY CROWDED PLACE?
COME ON! IT'S NOT THAT BAD!
YEAH! WE CAN DO LOTS OF NICE THINGS!

NO! I MISS OUR COZY HOUSE! OUR SUPERB PASTIMES!
!

I MISS MY BOOKS, MY POEMS, OUR CUTE TEA-TABLE WITH ITS LITTLE CHAIRS...
ARGH! IS HE GONNA COMPLAIN FOR THE WHOLE WEEKEND?!

MAYBE WE COULD... PSST PSST...
GOOD IDEA!

JUST GIVE US SOME TIME! WE HAVE A SPECIAL PROGRAM FOR YOU!
HUH?!

SCRIPT: TEA ORSI; LAYOUT: LUCA USAI; INK: MICHELA FRARE; COLOUR: LUCIO DE GIUSEPPE

LATER..
AT LAST! YOU'RE BACK!
PLEASE, FOLLOW ME TO THE CATERPILLAR GALLERY!

HUH?! WHAT IS IT?
YOU'LL SEE!

WELCOME TO OUR ART EXHIBITION!
OH! IT'S AMAZING!
I'LL BE YOUR GUIDE!

I WANT TO KNOW EVERY SINGLE DETAIL ABOUT THESE BEAUTIFUL PAINTINGS!
AHEM... SURE!

AFTER A LONG VISIT...
THANK YOU, THAT WAS MARVELOUS!
AND THE BEST IS STILL TO COME!
AS WE PREPARE THE NEXT EVENT, YOU CAN ENJOY A BEAUTY TREATMENT!
FANTASTIC! THIS IS JUST WHAT ACTORS LIKE ME LOVE!
AND WHEN THE TREATMENT'S OVER...
PLEASE, BE OUR GUEST!
ISN'T THIS THE POSHEST TEA PARTY YOU'VE EVER HAD?!
IT IS INDEED!
WE CAN TALK ABOUT POETRY AND THEATRE AND...
SIGH! AND AFTER THIS WE EVEN HAVE THE PLAY!

SO... HAVE YOU CHANGED YOUR MIND ABOUT SUNNYSIDE?

DEFINITELY! THE TOYS HERE ARE QUITE SOPHISTICATED! I LIKE THEM!

I CAN'T WAIT TO SEE WHAT YOU'VE IN STORE FOR TOMORROW!

ARGH!

COME ON! AT LEAST HE'S NOT COMPLAINING NOW! HEE, HEE!

THE END

# SAME AIM – DIFFERENT MEANS

SCRIPT: TEA ORSI; LAYOUT: GIANFRANCO FLORIO; INK: MICHELA FRARE; COLOUR: LUCIO DE GIUSEPPE

SOON THE TOYS SPLIT INTO TWO GROUPS ...
TRIXIE'S RIGHT! E-CARDS ARE COOL AND FULL OF SPECIAL EFFECTS!
NOT AT ALL! A HAND-WRITTEN CARD SHOWS THAT YOU REALLY CARE!
FOLKS?!
HEY! WHAT IF WE MAKE TWO CARDS?!
GOOD IDEA!
BUT WE'RE ALL FRIENDS! WE SHOULD SEND ONE SINGLE CARD FROM US ALL!
BUT AS WE CAN'T AGREE WE'D BETTER SPLIT INTO TWO GROUPS!
OKAY, THEN I'LL WORK WITH BOTH!
FIRST, WOODY JOINS THE E-CARD GROUP ...
HMM... CAN'T YOU FIND SOMETHING LIKE "SHOE CELEBRATIONS"?
LOVE
GOOD LUCK
BIRTHDAY CARDS
UHM...
NO! IT DOESN'T SEEM TO BE A VERY COMMON OCCASION!
MAYBE YOU CAN FIND A GIRLY BIRTHDAY CARD WITH SHOES ON IT!
GOOD LUCK
SURE! LET'S TRY!
BIRTHDAY

IN FACT, AFTER A LONG SEARCH ...
ISN'T IT TOO PINK?
DON'T WORRY, BUDDY! KEN WILL LOVE IT!
Best Wishes
THANKS FOR HELPING US, WOODY!
YOU'RE WELCOME! I'M GONNA CHECK ON THE OTHER GROUP NOW!
ONE MINUTE LATER, IN BONNIE'S ROOM ...
WHAT SHALL WE DRAW?
HOW ABOUT A PAIR OF TRENDY SHOES?
NO! WE SHOULD WRITE A SPECIAL POEM!
A SHOE IS A SHOE AND A TREAT FOR YOUR FOOT...
AHEM... CAN I GIVE YOU SOME ADVICE!
MAYBE YOU COULD ...

LATER, WHEN THE CARDS ARE READY ...
OKAY! YOU'VE DONE A GREAT JOB! SO SHOW EACH OTHER YOUR CARDS!
YES! YES! LET'S SEE THEM!
SURPRISE!
HUH?! THEY LOOK SO SIMILAR!
YEAH! THEY'RE BOTH GALACTIC!
YOU SEE? EVEN THOUGH YOU SPLIT UP, YOU HAD THE SAME IDEA!
Best Wishes
Best Wishes
I BET WOODY KNEW THIS WOULD HAPPEN ALL ALONG!!
WELL... MAYBE...
I WONDER WHAT KEN AND BARBIE WILL SAY WHEN THEY GET TWO CARDS...
NEXT MORNING...
WHY DID THEY MAKE TWO IDENTICAL CARDS?
WELL... MAYBE ONE WASN'T ENOUGH FOR OUR SUPER COOL SHOES!
Best Wishes
Best Wishes
THE END

# A FASHION SURPRISE

Disney · Pixar TOY STORY 3

SCRIPT: TEO ORSI, PENCIL: GIANFRANCO FLORIO, INK: MICHELA FRARE, COLOR: ANGELA CAPOLUPO

THE NEXT DAY
I GUESS IT'S TOO SMALL NOW...
URGH!
IT'S IMPOSSIBLE TO GET THE RIGHT SIZE IF I CAN'T MEASURE BARBIE!
LET'S ASK HER TO COME HERE!
WE CAN'T!
IT'S A SURPRISE!
BUT MAYBE WE CAN ASK KEN TO CHANGE THE GIFT A BIT...
?
NEXT DAY
THIS SUPER TAILOR WILL CREATE A BEAUTIFUL DRESS JUST FOR YOU!
DOLLY! HOW GREAT!
THE END

# THE STORM TEST

TOY STORY 3

LOOK! THE FORECAST SAYS THERE'S A BIG STORM COMING!

A STORM! EVERYBODY GET READY FOR THE STORM TEST!
OH NO...

STORM TEST?
IT'S A SPECIAL TEST BUZZ SET UP SOME YEARS AGO...

"...THE DAY WE ALMOST LOST A TOY IN A STORM!"
HELP! I'M FLYING AWAY!

IT'S FOR OUR OWN SAFETY, DOLLY...
AND WHAT IS IT EXACTLY?

SCRIPT: ALESSANDRO FERRARI, PENCIL & INKS: VALENTINO FORLINI, COLOR: ANGELA CAPOLUPO

IT'S SIMPLE, YOU JUST HAVE TO GO INSIDE THE WIND TUNNEL...

"...WAIT FOR WHEN BUZZ TURNS IT ON FULL-SPEED...

"...AND IF YOU CAN'T STAY STILL..."
AHHH!

"...TEST FAILED!"
THUMP

"SO YOU NEED SOMETHING TO WEIGH YOU DOWN"
SIGH...
I NEVER PASS THAT TEST WHEN I'M EMPTY!
A RANGER IS ALWAYS PREPARED!

THE END

# SAND MISSION

Disney·PIXAR
TOY STORY 3
BONNIE'S ROOM. THE TOYS ARE RECREATING A HAWAIIAN VACATION FOR KEN AND BARBIE!
NOW WE NEED THE SAND. I'LL ASK BUZZ...

WHERE IS HE?
LAST TIME I SAW HIM, HE WAS PRACTICING WITH THE GLOW STICKS...
YOU DON'T NEED BUZZ, WOODY! WE CAN DO THAT!

"I HAVE A PLAN!"
WHAT ARE WE DOIN' HERE, JESSIE? IT'S FREEZING!
OUR TARGET IS THE SANDBOX IN THE NEIGHBORS' GARDEN, REX! THERE WE'LL FIND WHAT WE NEED...

YEAH, BUT... WHERE IS IT, COWGIRL?
DON'T WORRY, HAMM, I'VE A MAP OF THE GARDEN!

SCRIPT: ALESSANDRO FERRARI; LAYOUT: VALENTINO FORLINI; INK: VALENTINO FORLINI; COLOUR: LUCIO DE GIUSEPPE

I BET WE WON'T MAKE IT.
BET ACCEPTED. I FEEL LUCKY TODAY –

WHUMP

FORGET IT. YOU WON, HAMM.
DON'T EVEN THINK ABOUT IT! I HAVE A PLAN!

ANOTHER ONE?!
MOUNT ON REX'S SHOULDERS, HAMM!

I'M TOO FULL OF COINS FOR THIS!
BUTTERCUP! MOUNT ON HAMM'S!
I'M TOO SOFT FOR THIS!

YES! IT'S WORKING! TEN STEPS AHEAD AND WE'RE THERE!
TEN STEPS? I DON'T KNOW IF I CAN MAKE IT EVEN FOR JUST ONE OR TWO, JESSIE!

JUST TO KNOW... WHAT WILL WE DO WHEN WE'LL REACH THE SANDBOX?

WE DIG.

SO...
C'MON! IT'S HERE! WE FOUND IT!

UH-OH...
THUNK

IT'S... FROZEN!
WHAT? NO!
YUP! LIKE A GLASS OF WATER AT THE NORTH POLE! WELL DONE, MISS "I HAVE A PLAN!"

WORST MISSION EVER!
THE WORST THING IS THAT WE DON'T HAVE THE SAND FOR KEN AND BARBIE...

DON'T WORRY, JESSIE. BUZZ HAS SAVED THE DAY...

...WITH A LITTER BOX!
THE CAT'S LITTER BOX?!
THAT'S PERFECT! WHY DIDN'T WE THINK ABOUT IT?

BECAUSE HE'S A SPACE RANGER, PIGGY BANK!
HEY! ANYBODY?

COULD YOU HELP ME?
SORRY, I'M NOT A SPACE RANGER!
THE END

# TOY GAMES

DISNEY · PIXAR
TOY STORY 3

AT BONNIE'S HOUSE THE TOYS RECEIVE UNEXPECTED NEWS...

THE SUNNYSIDE TOYS HAVE INVITED US TO PARTICIPATE IN THE FALL TOY GAMES NEXT SATURDAY?

BUT WE'LL NEVER BE ABLE TO WIN!

BUT WE HAVE A REAL SPACE RANGER! WE CAN WIN!
YES, WE CAN!

I'LL GIVE YOU LESSONS! I'LL TRAIN YOU! AND IN JUST ONE WEEK...


SCRIPT: ALESSADNRO FERRARI, PENCILS: LUCA USAI, INK: MICHELA FRARE,COLOR: ANGELA CAPOLUPO

"...YOU'LL BE CHAMPIONS IN RUNNING..."
REX? WHAT ARE YOU DOING?
I WANT TO KNOW EVERYTHING ABOUT SPORTS, COACH LIGHTYEAR!
SPORTS RULES

"...RIDING OBSTACLE COURSE..."
NO! YOU MUST JUMP OVER THE OBSTACLE!

"...WEIGHTLIFTING..."
MAYBE IT'S BETTER TO START OFF EASY, WOODY...

"...AND SWIMMING!"
SIGH...

OKAY, WE STILL HAVE SIX DAYS!

THANKS TO BUZZ'S PERSEVERANCE...
WOW! I LOVE BADMINTON!

...AFTER A VERY LONG WEEK OF TRAINING...
GREAT JUMP, BULLSEYE!

...THE TOYS ARE READY FOR THE GAMES!

READY?

GOOOOO!

BUT...
I'M SORRY, BUZZ... THE FALL TOY GAMES GOT CANCELLED BECAUSE OF THE SNOW!
OH NO...
WHY DID I LEARN EVERYTHING ABOUT BADMINTON THEN?

WAIT A SECOND...
YOU SAID SNOW, TRIXIE?
YES...
WHY?

FASTER!
FASTER!
THE WINTER
TOY GAMES ARE
COMING UP!

THERE ARE WINTER TOY
GAMES TOO? CAN'T WE WAIT
FOR NEXT FALL?
BUT I WAS
JUST GETTING GOOD
AT BADMINTON!

THE END

Toy Story 3

# WINTER SPORTS

THE END

SCRIPT: ALESSANDRO SISTI; LAYOUT & INK: LUCA USAI; COLOUR: LUCIO DE GIUSEPPE

# JINGLE BELLS

Disney · PIXAR
TOY STORY 3

CHRISTMAS IS NEAR!
BEHOLD! SNOWFLAKES ARE FLOATING DOWN AND... HUH?
JINGLE JINGLE

HAMM! I'M TRYING TO WRITE A POEM! COULD YOU PLEASE BE QUIET!
AHEM! OKAY... I'LL TRY!

BUT...
JINGLE JINGLE JINGLE
HOW RUDE!

I ASKED YOU TO BE QUIET AND NOW YOU'RE MAKING EVEN MORE NOISE!
LISTEN! I'D REALLY LIKE TO DO AS YOU ASK BUT I CAN'T!

IT'S NOT MY FAULT! BONNIE DRESSED ME UP FOR CHRISTMAS!
JINGLE JINGLE JINGLE
OH MY!
THE END

SCRIPT: TEA ORSI, LAYOUT: VALENTINO FORLINI, INK: VALENTINO FORLINI, COLOUR: ANGELA CAPOLUPO

# A SNOWY MISSION

DISNEY · PIXAR
TOY STORY 3
BONNIE'S AT THE DAYCARE AND...
OH, NO!
?!
WHAT'S UP, JESSIE?

THAT BIRD SEEMS SO HUNGRY!
YEAH! I GUESS IT'S HARD TO FIND FOOD IN THE SNOW!

WE MUST HELP HIM, WOODY!
MMM...

WE COULD GET SOME CRUMBS FROM THE BREAD BOX AND THEN FEED THE BIRD!
THAT'S A GALACTIC PLAN, BUDDY!

SCRIPT: TEA ORSI; LAYOUT & INK: VALENTINO FORLINI; COLOUR: ANGELA CAPOLUPO

IN THE KITCHEN...
ARE YOU READY, GUYS?
YEAH! DROP THE BREAD CRUMBS!

HERE YOU GO!
HEY! YOU'VE GOT TO DROP THEM INTO THE BAG, BUZZ!
ARGH!

SOME CRUMBS LATER...
SO! WHAT'S THE NEXT STEP?
WE'VE GOT TO TAKE THE FOOD TO THE BIRD!

BUT...
HOLD ON!
WHAT?!

I DON'T WANT TO GET **WET!**
HUH?! ME NEITHER!

WE NEED SOME **WATERPROOF** GARMENTS!
SURE! LET'S GO BACK INSIDE!

TA-DA!
?!
WHAT DO YOU WANT TO DO WITH THAT **PLASTIC WRAP?**
YOU'LL FIND OUT SOON!
BLINK

IN FACT...
HOPEFULLY NO ONE WILL SEE US!
**COME ON!** THE BIRD IS WAITING!

PANT! I DIDN'T THINK IT WAS SO HARD TO WALK IN THE SNOW!
YEAH! LET'S STOP HERE!

NEXT STEP: SPREADING THE CRUMBS!
LOOK! THE BIRD IS COMING CLOSER!
CHIRP!

AND...
YAWN!
FINALLY WE CAN GO BACK INSIDE AND GET SOME REST!
AHEM... YEAH...

CHIRP
BUT FIRST WE'VE GOT TO FEED SOME MORE FRIENDS!
CHIRP
CHIRP
CHIRP
GASP!
HUH?!
THE END

# SPACE COMEDY

Disney · PIXAR TOY STORY 3

THAT NIGHT, KEN AND CHUNK ARRIVED AT BONNIE'S HOUSE ON A GARBAGE TRUCK...

AND... ACTION!

THEY SECRETLY BORROWED THE SUNNYSIDE CAMERA TO SHOOT A MOVIE!

JESSIE WANTS TO GIVE A SPECIAL PRESENT TO BUZZ... A SHORT MOVIE FULL OF SPACE ADVENTURES!
JESSIE AND THE ALIENS ARE THE MAIN CHARACTERS!

MR. PRICKLEPANTS IS THE DIRECTOR!
AND... ACTION!

REX IS THE ALIEN MONSTER!
UH? G-GROAR!

WHILE KEN TAKES CARE OF THE CAMERA!
AND OF THE COSTUMES!

PRE 34495 SCRIPT: ALESSANDRO FERRARI; LAYOUT & INK: VALENTINO FORLINI; COLOUR: MARA DAMIANI & ANGELA CAPOLUPO

BUT THINGS DON'T GO EXACTLY AS JESSIE HAD PLANNED...
JESSIE THE SPACE IS IN DANGER! WE NEED THE HELP OF OUR HERO...
THE CLAW!

STOP! WHO IS THIS CLAW? IT'S NOT IN THE SCRIPT!

YOU HAVE TO SAY "BUZZ LIGHTYEAR"!
THE CLAW!

SIGH! LET'S MOVE TO THE NEXT SCENE...

NEXT SCENE? STOP! CHANGE OF COSTUMES!

ALREADY? WE ONLY JUST STARTED!
A PROFESSIONAL NEVER WEARS THE SAME COSTUME IN TWO DIFFERENT SCENES!
THESE ARE THE ONES WE TOOK FROM SUNNYSIDE... JUST FOR THE FIRST THREE SCENES!
W-WE HAVE TO WEAR ALL THESE?! BUT WE'LL NEVER MAKE IT...
EXCUSE ME, IS IT MY TURN?
WATCH OUT, REX! YOU'RE...
THUMP
WHAM

HELP ME OUT!
YOU'RE RUINING MY SPECIAL SURPRISE!
IM SORRY! I DIDN'T MEAN TO!

THE END
THE CLAW!

NEXT DAY, JESSIE JUST SHOWED BUZZ THE MOVIE...
I'M SO SORRY, I WANTED TO GIVE YOU AN ADVENTURE MOVIE, AND INSTEAD...
THE END

IT'S THE FUNNIEST COMEDY I'VE EVER SEEN INSTEAD!
HAHAHA!

THANK YOU, JESSIE! I LIKE IT A LOT!
SMACK
IT WAS THE PERFECT PRESENT! JESSIE HAS TO THANK HER FRIENDS... FOR BEING SUCH DISASTERS!
THE END

# HERO OF THE DAY

SCRIPT: ALESSANDRO FERRARI, PENCILS: GIANFRANCO FLORIO, INK: MICHELA FRARE, COLOR: ANGELA CAPOLUPO

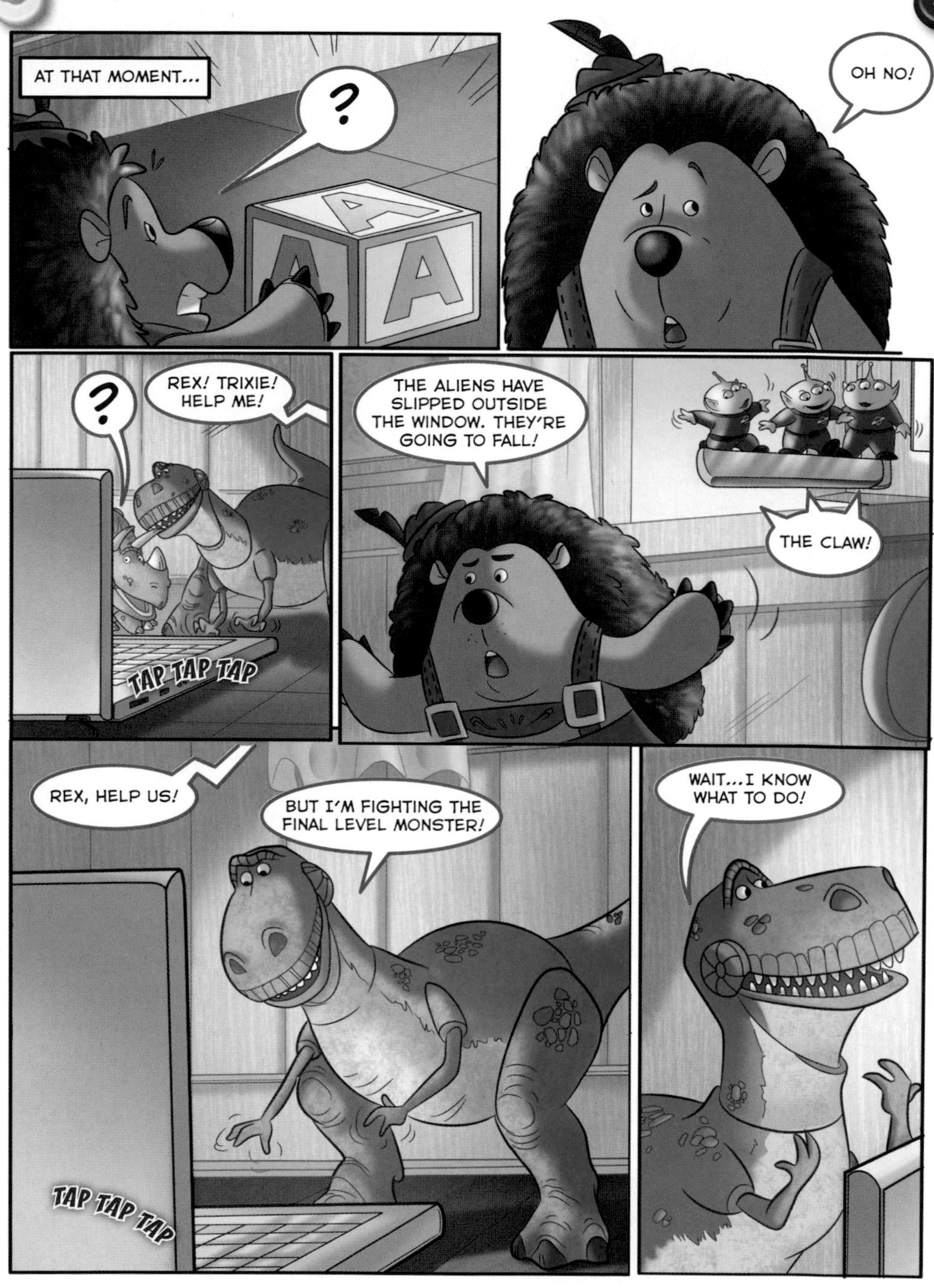
AT THAT MOMENT...
?
OH NO!
?
REX! TRIXIE! HELP ME!
TAP TAP TAP
THE ALIENS HAVE SLIPPED OUTSIDE THE WINDOW. THEY'RE GOING TO FALL!
THE CLAW!
REX, HELP US!
BUT I'M FIGHTING THE FINAL LEVEL MONSTER!
TAP TAP TAP
WAIT...I KNOW WHAT TO DO!

REX?
I'M COMING, TRIXIE!
TAP TAP TAP

WHAT ARE YOU DOING?
I'M ABOUT TO BEAT THE MONSTER...AND SAVE OUR FRIENDS...
TAP TAP TAP

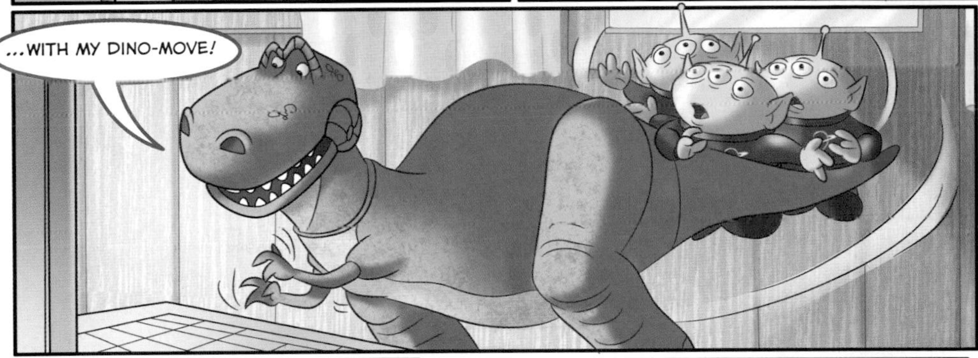
...WITH MY DINO-MOVE!

OHHH

OH NO! THE FINAL MONSTER'S JUST KILLED ME! I'LL NEVER BE THE HERO OF DINO-HERO!
GAME OVER
MAYBE, BUT YOU'RE OUR HERO NOW!
OOOOH!

THE END

# THE SPACE-RODEO

BONNIE'S AWAY FOR THE WEEKEND AND HAS BROUGHT WOODY, BULLSEYE AND DOLLY WITH HER...
I THINK JESSIE MISSES BONNIE!
SIGH!

YEAH, BUT SHE'LL BE BACK SOON.

BUT WE SHOULD TRY CHEERING HER UP!
HOW?

I'LL ORGANIZE A SURPRISE RODEO TO MAKE HER SMILE AGAIN!
HURRAY!

LET'S TALK TO WOODY AND BULLSEYE!
AHEM... BUZZ...

WOODY AND BULLSEYE ARE WITH BONNIE, REMEMBER?!
WELL... NOTHING CAN STOP BUZZ LIGHTYEAR! LET'S GET TO WORK!

SCRIPT: ALESSANDRO FERRARI, PENCIL: GIANFRANCO FLORIO, INK: MICHELA FRARE, COLOR: ANGELA CAPOLUPO

OKAY, JESSIE WILL SIT THERE AND YOU'LL PUSH HER...
THIS DOESN'T LOOK LIKE A RODEO, BUZZ!

I KNOW, BUT I CAN'T MAKE A RODEO WITHOUT A RODEO HORSE, AND...
CAN I PLAY?
AHEM... SURE!
A MINUTE LATER...
YIHAAAA!
WROOOM
THANK YOU, BUZZ! YOU'RE THE BEST!
!
THE END

# IT'S BEDTIME

DISNEY PIXAR TOY STORY 3

SIGH, THE PEAS ARE SO NOISY!
WE'LL NEVER BE ABLE TO WATCH THE SHOW...
WHOAAA!
BOING BOING BOING

DON'T WORRY, I'LL READ A BEDTIME STORY AND MAKE THEM SLEEPY!

IN FACT...
...AND THEY LIVED HAPPILY EVER AFTER.
ZZZ

GREAT! NOW WE CAN WATCH THE SHOW IN PEACE.
ZIIIP

BUT...
I GUESS MY STORY WORKED TOO WELL.
ZZZZZZZ
THE END

SCRIPT: TEA ORSI, PENCIL: ANDREA GREPPI, INK: MICHELA FRARE, COLOR: LUCIO DE GIUSEPPE

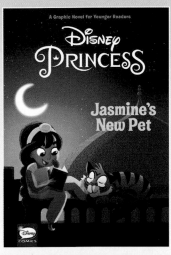